The Dragon Daughter

and Other

Lin Lan Fairy Tales

ODDLY MODERN FAIRY TALES

Jack Zipes, *Series Editor*

Oddly Modern Fairy Tales is a series dedicated to publishing unusual literary fairy tales produced mainly during the first half of the twentieth century. International in scope, the series includes new translations, surprising and unexpected tales by well-known writers and artists, and uncanny stories by gifted yet neglected authors. Postmodern before their time, the tales in *Oddly Modern Fairy Tales* transformed the genre and still strike a chord.

The Dragon Daughter

and Other

Lin Lan Fairy Tales

Edited and translated by Juwen Zhang

With a foreword by Jack Zipes

PRINCETON UNIVERSITY PRESS   *Princeton and Oxford*

Published by Princeton University Press
41 William Street, Princeton, New Jersey 08540
6 Oxford Street, Woodstock, Oxfordshire OX20 1TR

press.princeton.edu

All Rights Reserved
ISBN (pbk.) 9780691214412
ISBN (e-book) 9780691225067

British Library Cataloging-in-Publication Data is available

Editorial: Anne Savarese and James Collier
Production Editorial: Sara Lerner
Text and Cover Design: Pamela L. Schnitter
Production: Erin Suydam
Publicity: Alyssa Sanford and Carmen Jimenez
Copyeditor: Jennifer Harris

Cover art by Andrea Dezsö

This book has been composed in Adobe Jenson Pro

Printed on acid-free paper. ∞

Printed in the United States of America

10 9 8 7 6 5 4 3 2 1

■ Contents

■ List of Illustrations

■ Acknowledgments

The tales in this little book, nearly a hundred years after they were published in Chinese, would not have come alive in English without support and help from many individuals. Among them, I want to particularly thank Professor Xiao Fang and Dr. Jia Chen at Beijing Normal University, Professor Liu Xiaochun at Sun Yatsen University, and Professor Liu Shouhua at Central China Normal University for helping find references. I thank Dr. Bill Long of Salem, Oregon, for providing many constructive suggestions about my translations and writings on the topic. If readers find joy in reading the tales here, it is owing to the painstaking work and professional dedication from the editorial team for this book. For that, I sincerely thank all the editors, as well as the anonymous reviewers. To my wife, Jing; and our children, Andy and Teddy, who supported me with time and daily delights, my gratitude goes beyond words. Most of all, without the encouragement of Jack Zipes as a mentor and a friend, I would not even have started this project; without his careful and thoughtful proofreading, this little book would not read as it does now, and I thank him from the bottom of my heart.

■ Foreword

JACK ZIPES

Juwen Zhang's *The Dragon Daughter and Other Lin Lan Fairy Tales* is a stunning, revolutionary book. It is stunning because, to my knowledge, few folklorists and literary critics in the world are aware that the Lin Lan tales ever existed. These stories, highly popular in China in the early twentieth century, combined elements from European fairy tales with traditional oral Chinese narratives. They are revolutionary not because they adhered to a particular ideology, but because a small group of writers wanted to produce something "modern" and joined together to create intriguing stories often more mysterious and Kafkaesque than Kafka's tales.

As Zhang points out, the development of the Lin Lan, Lady Lin Lan, tales emerged during the Sinification and modernist movement in China from 1920 to 1940, when the Chinese adapted many cultural art forms from the West to awaken self-awareness of and self-confidence in their own traditions and rituals. A group of writers at the Shanghai publishing house North New Books published 43 volumes with close to one thousand tales gathered from informants all over China. In this regard, the editors of the Lin Lan tales were similar to the Brothers Grimm, and certainly they were familiar with the Grimms' tales, but the dominant motifs and characters in their stories derived from Chinese folklore. The publication of the series lasted until the late 1930s, influencing children and adults for more than twenty years.

The significance of the Lin Lan tales cannot be understated. In fact, these unusual narratives cannot be simply catalogued as fairy tales, but represent a range of genres: Chinese legends, comic tales, ghost stories, fables, and folk tales called *tonghua* that reflect polytheistic traditions. The combination of these tales with elements of Western folk and fairy tales make the Lin Lan tales all the more alluring, for it is clear that many if not most of the tales can be explained only if one studies the Chinese and European roots and sources of the narrative.

Clearly, the Lin Lan tales are enigmatic, magical, and fabulous. They are beyond definition and abide by their own laws. One thing is clear, however: the Lin Lan tales have not lost their appeal, for the more our own world becomes unfathomable, the more these hybrid tales resonate with conditions we currently face.

Zhang has provided only a tiny selection of the hundreds of Lin Lan tales, and thanks to his endeavors, we now have a better understanding of how and why oddly modern fairy tales have developed throughout the world. Whether oral or written, metaphorical tales in all countries enable us to gain distance from our lives even as they speak to our needs and desires. What is fascinating about this collection is that cultural differences make no difference whatsoever when storytellers from different countries weld them into universal mysteries.

The Dragon Daughter

and Other

Lin Lan Fairy Tales

Rediscovering Fairy Tales in China

Unknown in English-speaking countries, the small selection of Lin Lan tales presented here is intended to fill a gap in the international history of folk and fairy tales. In the past century or so, folklorists and fairy-tale scholars in many countries have demonstrated how widespread the influence of the Brothers Grimm has been throughout the world. If we consider that there were "Brothers Grimm" in virtually every country of the West in the nineteenth century—for example, Peter Christen Asbjørnsen and Jorgen Moe in Norway, Elias Lönnrot in Finland, Hans Christian Andersen and Sven Grundtvig in Denmark, Vuk Karadzic in Serbia, Božena Němcová in Czechoslovakia, Alexander Afanasyev in Russia, Adolfo Cœlho in Portugal, Emmanuel Cosquin in France, and Giuseppe Pitrè in Italy—it is not surprising to see a similar development in early twentieth-century China—namely, the Lin Lan tales.

The emergence of Lin Lan as the Grimms of China, however, has rarely been studied or explored inside or outside China (Zhang 2020). Consequently, this introduction is intended to provide a sociohistorical context for understanding the development of the Lin Lan tales.

The pseudonym "Lin Lan," created on July 12, 1924, was first used as a pen name by one author, Li Xiaofeng, who published a set of literary stories about a legendary figure in Chinese history. The success of these stories eventually led the author to work on the newly imported "genre" of fairy tales (*tonghua*, 童话), and he was later joined by several other editors and writers who shared the pen name "Lin Lan" (林兰) or "Lady Lin Lan" (林兰女士) for collecting and publishing a series of fairy tales from different parts of China.

The Lin Lan Series was published from the late 1920s to the early 1930s by North New Books (*beixin shuju*) in Shanghai, which also published many important works by the leading literary figures at that time, including Lu Xun (鲁迅, 1881–1936). The series was divided into three subgenres: *minjian chuanshuo* (folk legends and tales), *minjian tonghua* (folk fairy tales), and *minjian qushi* (comic folk tales), with a total of 43 volumes containing nearly one thousand tales. All of the tales were provided by informants, who collected the tales from oral storytellers in different parts of China in response to a call from the publisher, as the Brothers Grimm did in 1815. Each volume was about one hundred pages, containing approximately twenty tales. Many of these volumes were reprinted, sometimes several times, indicating that most of the children in urban schools were familiar with these tales in the early part of the twentieth century.

Eight volumes out of the series were categorized as "folk fairy tales." The concept of "fairy tale" was introduced to China at the turn of the twentieth century, along with such terms as "folklore" and "nationalism." This concept was then further developed through the translation of fairy tales or *Märchen* from Europe; the publication of tales collected in China; and the creation of Chinese *tonghua* imitating the form of European fairy tales with content adapted from Chinese tales.

In 1909, *tonghua* was first used in China as the title of a series of publications, edited by Sun Yuxiu (孙毓修, 1871–1922), in which

European fairy tales served as examples of the literary tradition. Sun thus created a new category in publications and library catalogues. Today, Sun Yuxiu is heralded as the father of "Chinese *tonghua*." His ultimate goal was to promote "children's education," as other intellectuals and writers had done, such as Zhou Zuoren (周作人, 1885–1967), who introduced the term *minsu* (folklore; folk customs) to China in 1913, and who translated fairy tales by Oscar Wilde, Hans Christian Andersen, the Brothers Grimm, and other authors in the 1910s.

By the 1920s, *tonghua* became widely accepted as a new genre of literature (that is, folk literature). During this period, leading Chinese scholars absorbed ideas and influences from both Europe and Japan. Both Lu Xun and his younger brother Zhou Zuoren spent some years in Japan and knew the leading Japanese folklorists. As a result of their work, the efforts of the extensive New Culture Movement made people more aware of Chinese folk literature. In particular, *tonghua* produced by Chinese writers were gradually accepted and welcomed by large segments of Chinese.

In addition to the great popularity of the series, there are three significant reasons that "Lin Lan" should be regarded as "the Grimms of China": (1) the influence of the Grimms on the Lin Lan Series; (2) the exemplary dedication of the series to the oral tradition of the lower classes; and (3) the social and literary impact in historical perspective.

When the Brothers Grimm began to collect folk and fairy tales with a clear goal of searching for the true voice of the folk and the pride of their culture and history, the Prussian-dominated German Empire was in a crisis that eventually led to the establishment of the German Confederation (1815). It was during the rise of Germany as a nation-state that the first edition of *Kinder- und Hausmärchen*

(*Children's and Household Tales*) was published (1812–1815), which doubtlessly helped create support for a unified nation.

In this sense, the Grimms developed what can be called "the Brothers Grimm spirit." As Jack Zipes has written, "the Grimms hoped to find great truth about the German people and their laws and customs by collecting their tales, for they believed that language was what created national bonds and stamped the national character of a people" (Zipes 1987: xxviii). This spirit was also part of a romantic nationalism that was characteristic of German ideas in the eighteenth and nineteenth centuries. It was this spirit that became a driving force for many countries seeking to maintain their cultural traditions by establishing the sources and roots of a national culture. It was precisely for this reason that the Lin Lan phenomenon took place in China in the early twentieth century.

The effort to record oral tales from storytellers—that is, the common people—was the principle behind the Lin Lan Series, more so than in other similar collections published in China. There is clear evidence that the Lin Lan creators, like the literati at that time, knew a good deal about the Brothers Grimm's 1815 letter "Circular wegen der Aufsammlung der Volkspoesie" (Circular-Letter Concerned with Collecting of Folk Poetry), along with the second volume of the first edition of *Kinder- und Hausmärchen*, which recognized the status of ordinary storytellers and the scope of their efforts to collect tales. In this sense, the Lin Lan Series was exemplary.

Even from a contemporary viewpoint, the Lin Lan Series has contributed greatly to the continuity of the oral and literary traditions in China, linking the previous oral and written records to those that are retold today. Tale-type and motif studies demonstrate that the fairy tales in the Lin Lan Series not only mediated

4

between the oral and literary traditions but also stimulated the rise of Chinese *tonghua*. For example, the publication of the best-known indigenous *tonghua*, *The Strawman* (*Daocaoren*, 1922) by Ye Shengtao (叶圣陶, 1894–1988), marked the first success of Sinification under the influence of Andersen's "The Steadfast Tin Soldier."

While many others published folk and fairy tales in the early twentieth century in China, the Lin Lan Series emerged at a unique historical moment and played an essential role in the continuity of collecting and publishing folk and fairy tales at the time. This was owing to several factors. The first is that North New Books was perhaps the most influential publisher during the New Culture Movement, thus promoting modern literature. It published books by Lu Xun, considered the most prominent writer in twentieth-century China, and by his brother Zhou Zuoren, a key figure in the development of folklore and the fairy tale in China who also became a member of the Lin Lan team. The editor-in-chief of North New Books, Li Xiaofeng (李晓峰, 1897–1971), was Lu Xun's closest student and friend, and used Lin Lan as a pen name for some publications. Another factor is the content of the fairy tales and their role in the transmission of the oral and literary traditions in China.

Important social and economic factors also contributed to the emergence of the Lin Lan phenomenon. The May Fourth Movement in 1919 certainly encouraged the Chinese to reflect on the domestic history that led to the "backwardness" of China. Chinese elites sought to advance the nation through a "new culture" (represented by Western science, technology, and ideas in contrast to the traditional Confucian values and lifestyle). The new vernacular speech (*baihua*, 白话) also promoted new ideas through publication.

The need for "the Brothers Grimm spirit" in China initiated the New Culture Movement, including the Ballads Movement. In the twenty-first century, a revival of academic interest in the Lin Lan phenomenon has resulted in efforts to safeguard the Intangible Cultural Heritage (ICH) and the reconstruction of China's national identity.

When the name Lin Lan first appeared in 1924, it clearly was the pen name of Li Xiaofeng, a student of philosophy at Beijing University, who graduated in 1923. He was one of the founders of a publishing house named New Wave Press (*xinchaoshe*). Soon after he published the literary stories mentioned here, he changed the name of the press to North New Books and moved to Shanghai. He continued using the pen name Lin Lan to publish other stories until 1925. At the same time, Zhao Jingshen (赵景深, 1902–1984), who was then a leading scholar of fairy-tale studies, became Li's business partner. In 1928, Li invited Zhao to come to Shanghai to work with him, and paid his travel expenses. In April 1930, Zhao married Li's younger sister, Li Xitong (李希同), and, in June, he became the editor-in-chief of North New Books.

Soon after Zhao arrived in Shanghai, he took charge of the designing and publishing of the Lin Lan Series. By then, he had already published some important works about *tonghua* and established himself as one of the genre's most important scholars. Indeed, it was through their common interest in *tonghua* that Li and Zhao began their close collaboration. For instance, one of their major accomplishments was the translation of the Grimms' *Kinder- und Hausmärchen* in 1932. Two years later, Zhao published his first book on drama, which marked a change in his research interests, and he never published anything on *tonghua* thereafter. This might be a key reason that the Lin Lan Series ended in 1933.

Working as a team, Li was initially the strategist and Zhao was the editor-in-chief, assisted by other editors. Based on this history and personal experience, folklorist Che Xilun, who was Zhao's student in the 1960s, reasoned that Lin Lan was the name used by Li and Zhao, along with others involved in the publication of the Lin Lan Series at North New Books. Che also recalled that Zhao once introduced Li's wife, Cai Shuliu (蔡漱六, 1900–?), to him as Lin Lan—partly because she also worked as an editor at North New Books, and partly because she embodied (Lady) Lin Lan herself. In fact, when the Lin Lan Series became popular, readers demanded to see Lin Lan, who was assumed to be a female based on the name, and Cai Shuliu was chosen to represent the fictional author in public. Decades later, Cai Shuliu confirmed that Li used the name Lin Lan and even suggested changing her name to Lady Lin Lan (*Lin Lan nüshi*).

Indeed, during the early twentieth century it was fashionable for Chinese elites to publish literary works with a female name or title. It seems reasonable to guess that, on certain occasions, Lin Lan was the name used by a team of two or more people, but on other occasions, Lin Lan was the pen name of one particular person in charge of editing a particular tale or collection.

Furthermore, some of the contributors to the Lin Lan Series were also editors and authors of other volumes of fairy tales published by North New Books. Sun Jiaxun, for example, contributed the tales "After Replacing the Heart" and "The Golden Pin," but as an editor also published other volumes of fairy tales for children in the 1930s.

To some extent, it is no longer as meaningful to identify which writers and editors were part of Lin Lan as to understand the symbolism of Lin Lan in promoting the fairy-tale genre in China and introducing European fairy tales to the Chinese, especially to young people growing up from the 1920s to the 1940s. The tales helped them to gain a sense of their cultural roots through unique Chinese tales that aroused national pride, and led many to fight in the Sino-Japanese War for national independence in the 1930s to 1940s.

The Brothers Grimm and the Grimms of China had many similarities—among them the spirit of creating a national identity, the principles of collecting folk and fairy tales, and the social and literary impact—but two differences deserve to be mentioned as well.

One difference concerns religion. The Brothers Grimm had clear religious sentiments. To a certain extent, as Jack Zipes writes, "Wilhelm Grimm (more than Jacob) revised and altered most of the tales over a period of approximately forty years to make them more graceful and suitable for children and a proper Christian upbringing" (Zipes 1987: xxviii). By contrast, Lin Lan, whether as an individual or a team, reflected an inclusive Chinese polytheist tradition. The editors were attached to modernism and nationalism almost as a faith, although some tales expressed Confucian ethical teaching and the Buddhist "karma" idea.

The other difference concerns the pivotal role of the projects themselves. The Grimms published, often for the first time, tales that were "a few hundred years old before they had been gathered and told by the Grimms' informants," passed down through oral tradition (Zipes 2013: xxiii). In contrast, most of the Lin Lan tales (or tale types) can be found in historical records and are still told in contemporary everyday life. The Lin Lan tales transmitted literary as well as oral tales and also played a particular role in promoting vernacular speech in the early twentieth century, even though the name of Lin Lan is little known today.

The foremost value of the Lin Lan Series lies in the preservation of tales from particular regions during a particular time in Chinese history. Besides the social and political impact, these tales bear the personal marks of the storytellers who kept them in their memory and told them for a purpose.

The history of collecting and publishing oral tales and songs dates back to some of the earliest extant documents in Chinese, such as *The Book of Songs* (*Shijing*, ca. eleventh century to sixth century BCE), a collection of folk songs, and *The Classic of Mountains and Seas* (*Shanhaijing*, ca. third century BCE to third century CE), a collection of myths. These classics recorded many popular myths, fables, jokes, tales, and legends that often were used as analogies for political advice. From then on, folk tales were written down or compiled in each dynasty in Chinese history, forming a literary instead of an oral tradition.

In the long history of collecting tales, a few collections are of special relevance to this book. *Youyang Zazu*, a thirty-volume collection produced by Duan Chengshi (段成式, 803–863), categorized its tales by such genres as *zhiguai* (strange/wonder/ghost tales) and *nuogao*, a Daoist term for summoning ghosts and spirits, including the Chinese "Cinderella" tale (Ye Xian, 叶限) ATU510A, first introduced to the West by R. D. Jameson (1932).

Another collection, *Yi Jian Zhi* by Hong Mai (洪迈, 1123–1202), which contains more than 2,700 tales, is one of many literary collections or anthologies that demonstrate the continuing history of collecting and publishing tales in China. Approximately one hundred of its tales can be defined as complete folk tales or legends, including several tales about snake spirits that can be defined as fairy tales, which are also seen in the Lin Lan Series.

"The Snake Wife" is a common theme in Chinese folk and fairy tales, as seen in both the ancient records and the Lin Lan Series. Through extensive studies of Chinese and non-Chinese tales, however, folklorist Nai-tung Ting came to the conclusion that this type was initially formed in Western Asia or Central Asia, where there was no such practice as snake worship, and that it later entered India, Western Europe, and then China as a very common tale type or theme represented by "The Story of White Snake" (*baishe zhuan*) (Ting 1974; Liu 2017: 308–309). In this collection, "The Garden Snake" and "The Snake Spirit" are two variants of this tale type.

The tradition of collecting and publishing tales was greatly hampered during the eighteenth and nineteenth centuries in China, largely owing to wars and other social upheavals. The Lin Lan Series in the early twentieth century, along with the New Cultural Movement and the introduction of folklore and fairy tales in China, therefore played an important role in continuing that tradition.

The Sino-Japanese War and civil war in the 1930s to 1940s in China put an end to the rising trend of folklore studies of the 1920s and 1930s, but the establishment of the People's Republic of China in 1949 provided an opportunity for folklore studies to "serve the people." In 1957, the China Folk Literature and Art Society recommended that folklore studies should be continued as a part of the construction of the New China. A wave of collecting and publishing folk and fairy tales followed during the 1950s and 1970s, but it was limited to the "proletarian" working-class literature—that is, stories by workers and peasants praising the new society, along with a wave of translated Russian fairy tales. While the collection of local tales continued in many regions, tales often were edited or rewritten by the collectors. Other than these narratives, most traditional tales were labeled as "superstitious" and were suppressed in public life.

It was in this particular social context that the Lin Lan Series disappeared from public and academic life. Aside from ideological issues, there were practical factors: the New China after 1949 began to promote a new standard and simplified writing system (*jiantizi*) in order to let the common people learn to read and write. The format of printing in newspapers and books officially changed from a vertical line to a horizontal line, which eliminated the possibility of reprinting from previous editions of older books in mainland China. In Taiwan, however, the traditional writing (*fantizi*) and format of printing remained unchanged, which enabled the publication of two reprints of selected Lin Lan tales, in 1971 and 1981.

The reestablishment of the China Folklore Society in 1983 reflected a change of social and academic climate in China. From 1984 to 2009, the Ministry of Culture initiated the national project to publish the *Grand Collection of Folktales*, *Grand Collection of Ballads and Songs*, and *Grand Collection of Proverbs*. These three grand collections include 298 volumes at the provincial level and more than 4,000 volumes at the county level, along with numerous unpublished archival materials. Similar projects, though at a smaller scale, have been conducted with a focus on certain regions, historical periods, or themes.

Many tales in the Lin Lan Series are not only variants of the previous written records, as discussed earlier, but also directly related to oral storytelling. In addition, the tales reflect the many cultural differences between the tales of the Brothers Grimm and the tales of the Grimms of China. While many European fairy tales are related to hunting in forests, the Lin Lan series depicts agricultural life in China, with tales told in the rice fields or next to the stove. Protagonists in the Western tales are mostly hunters, traveling princes, or princesses asking questions, but those in Lin Lan's tales are mostly peasants, cooking girls transformed from garden snails or snakes, weavers, or dragon daughters who can build houses. The helpful creatures in Western tales are mostly forest animals like the wolf, the deer, or the eagle, but those in Lin Lan's tales are plowing cows, dogs, or domestic cats. In the Brothers Grimm tales, breaking taboos to obtain treasures reveals the spirit of the hunting culture, whereas in Lin Lan's tales breaking taboos is often related to losing treasure and credibility. Overall, the Lin Lan Series reflects the Chinese agricultural mentality and different values owing to different religious beliefs.

This present selection is intended to provide a complete and original picture of what the Lin Lan phenomenon signified in early twentieth-century China. Although the selection contains only about ten percent of the tales categorized as fairy tales in the Lin Lan Series, not to mention many tales from other categories, these tales indicate the richness and diversity of the oral and literary traditions in China.

The purpose of this collection is to restore the role of Lin Lan in the development or evolution of fairy tales in China, specifically in the 1920s and 1930s. It was the concept of the fairy tale that connected China to the West in form, particularly to the Brothers Grimm, as well as the nationalistic spirit in ideas behind the form.

The current collection thus highlights how fairy tales were understood, told, and discussed in China at that time. I have divided this collection into four parts to demonstrate similarities and differences between Chinese and European tales. For example, part 3, "The Hatred and Love of Siblings," shows the commonality among tales from all cultures, whereas part 2, "Predestined Love," represents Chinese notions of ghosts/souls as well as ethics and values concerning family. These tales were all selected from the original Lin Lan Series, which was published on a rolling schedule—as the tales were collected, they were roughly divided into fairy tales and legends and so on, and then published. (For more details, see the sections "Bibliographic Sources and Tale Types" and "Biographical Notes on Important Writers and Contributors," at the end of this book.)

The forty-two tales collected here are published for the first time in English, except for four included in a collection by Wolfram Eberhard (1937a), which I have retranslated. All of the translations are meant to be colloquial and to retain the flavor of the original Chinese stories. In my translating Chinese into English, whether classic and modern academic text or literary and everyday speech, I have followed two principles: (1) to be faithful to the meaning of the Chinese text, and (2) to adapt the Chinese style so that it resonates in English.

"Chinese" in this discourse refers essentially to the Chinese language—that is, all of the tales in the Lin Lan Series were told in Chinese (some were in dialects), and recorded or printed in Chinese (standard writing system), though the regions represented in the tales were mostly the provinces in South and Central China.

To ensure readability, I have tried to avoid footnotes or endnotes by either providing explanatory translations or adding annotative words in brackets. Some culturally distinctive expressions are translated to retain the original meaning with some "uniqueness," while avoiding direct association with the Western tradition. For example, in tale 6, the Chinese wanyinghe (万应盒, literally, "ten-thousand-answers box") and ruyibang (如意棒, literally, "as-you-wish stick") are translated respectively as "an All-Promise Box" and "an All-Wish Stick," although "magic box" and "magic wand" would make them more "familiar" to English readers. Some other examples are related to both cultural and textual issues.

Nearly a century after the Lin Lan Series was published seems to be a perfect time to recall the unusual tales that matched and, in some ways, surpassed the collection of the Brothers Grimm in quantity and cultural impact.

PART ONE

Love with a Fairy

民間童話集之四

林蘭編

1 ■ The Dragon Daughter

Many years ago, there were two brothers, one married, the other a bachelor. For some reason, the elder brother hated his younger brother, who was simple, honest, and loved playing music. As the years passed, the elder brother frequently told his wife that he wanted to get rid of his brother. Since his wife was a softhearted woman, she just listened to her husband, while each day, she saved a little bit of steamed bun and put it in a rickety old chest.

One night, the elder brother locked his younger brother into that rickety chest, dragged it to the river outside his house, and set it adrift down the river. Meanwhile, the younger brother, unconcerned, played his bamboo flute (*xiao*) inside the chest. Whenever he was hungry, he would eat some of the steamed buns.

As the chest drifted farther and farther, his music enchanted the Dragon King, who lived beneath the river. Soon, the king sent his guards to fetch the younger brother to his palace, where he played his flute for quite a long time, and everyone loved him. Whenever he played, even the fish and the tortoise kept quiet and listened. At the same time, he became friends with the guards, who revealed to him that, if he ever wanted to leave the palace, the Dragon King would offer him some gifts. But they also told him that he should decline all the gifts except for the little pet dog, who was not only the Dragon King's daughter but also the most beautiful woman in the world. Indeed, they explained that if he could ever manage to marry her, he would become the luckiest man in the world.

When the young man finally decided that it was time to leave the kingdom beneath the sea, the Dragon King insisted that he stay a few more days. Eventually, the Dragon King released him and offered him many gifts of jewelry, but the young man refused all the gifts. Somewhat taken aback, the Dragon King asked the young man whether there was anything in his palace he would like to take with him. The young man replied that he loved the little dog, and the Dragon King did not protest and let him take the dog with him, especially since he had nothing against the young musician. Once outside, the young man swam all the way to the water's surface with the dog on his back. As soon as they reached land, the little dog rolled on the ground, and, within a blink of an eye, the dog was transformed into a beautiful young woman. In fact, her beauty was simply indescribable and incomparable. Imagine how happy the young man was!

Now there was nothing left for them to do but to become husband and wife. But first they had to find a place to settle down. It might seem a shame that they were without a home, yet they were not concerned. They simply walked to a large lake, where they decided to build a house near the water. Of course, without people and money to help them, it seemed they would never succeed. Not to worry. The young woman smiled and said to her husband, "Go and take a rest!"

Therefore, he went and fell asleep in the woods nearby. When he woke up, he saw a splendid mansion in front of him. It was there that the couple lived and were content.

One day, when some of the local ministers were passing by the woods, they saw the large mansion and were astonished. How could such a mansion be standing there when the place had previously been a swamp? They went back to report to the king, who ordered the young man to come to the palace. The king gave him three days to build a large mansion in the palace courtyard. If he didn't finish the work by the end of the third day, the young man would be executed. Frightened, the young man went home and wept. After he told his wife what had happened, she smiled and told him not to cry any more, but to take a nap. She drew a mansion in the palace courtyard with her hand and blew on the drawing. All of a sudden, a magnificent mansion appeared in the palace courtyard! All the decorations and structures were much better than the king imagined they would be. What a pleasant surprise it was for the king!

Another time, there was a rebellion in the kingdom that had to be suppressed, but the king did not have enough soldiers to put down the rebellion. Consequently, he called the young man to his court and gave him three days to gather enough soldiers and horses to crush the rebellion. Once again, the young man went home crying. When his wife learned the truth, she smiled.

"Go and take a nap," she said. "There's no need for you to concern yourself about these affairs."

Then, she cut many paper stars in the room and blew them through the thin gaps of the windows. Soon, all the stars became soldiers and horses, and before long, they were so numerous that they covered a large field. They were then sent to fight, and after they put down the rebellion, the soldiers became the king's permanent army.

Not only was the king happy about the victory of his soldiers, but he was also amazed by the miracle. He summoned the young man and asked him how he had gained such magical powers. Since he was very honest, the young man told the king that it was his wife's power. When the king heard this news, he was so very delighted that he compelled the young man to send her to his palace, where she was to become the king's queen. Of course, it was impossible for the young man to say no to this demand. All he could do was to return home and weep. Soon after, several of the king's men arrived and commanded her to come with them.

His wife was not worried at all, and even told her husband not to be so sad. She told him that, after she left, he was to catch some birds and make a cloak out of their feathers. Once he did that, he was to wear the feather cloak and offer it for sale at the palace gate. Common people would not have enough money to buy it. If the king wanted to purchase the cloak, however, her husband was to demand the king's dragon robe in exchange. After that, she would take charge of their affairs. Once she finished telling him what to do, she got into the royal carriage and left.

The king was ecstatic when she arrived and threw parties every day in order to please her. But she became almost like a statue made of wood or clay and wouldn't speak a word or smile at all. The king tried every possible means to entertain her, but all his efforts were in vain.

One day, the king decided to hold a banquet for the queen at the golden palace. All the ministers arrived to entertain him and the queen. The queen, however, remained silent. Suddenly, someone began shouting outside and offered to sell a feather cloak. Upon hearing this, the queen smiled. The king also laughed and was delighted. He called in the man who was selling the feather cloak and decided to buy it. But the seller would not accept any offer unless the king would exchange it for the dragon robe. Even though the king was more powerful than the commoner, the king, at that time, could not force a commoner to sell something if he refused. In addition, in order to please the queen, the king did not want to make the situation embarrassing. He would do anything for the queen. So, the king finally decided to exchange his precious dragon robe for the cloak.

Once the exchange was made, the man who sold the feather cloak became the king and sat on the throne. Every one of the ministers cheered him and wished him a long, long life. All the guards came to protect him. All the people in the kingdom celebrated their new king. The first act of the new king and the queen was a command: "Remove the man wearing the feather cloak from the palace!"

Consequently, the former king was exiled and became a beggar because he had sought to possess another man's wife. The new royal couple lived happily ever after in the newly built palace courtyard. Peace reigned in the kingdom, and everyone appreciated the king and queen's magic powers.

2 ■ The Golden Pin

Once upon a time, there was a rugged mountain, and a young man by the name of Wang Er (second son of the Wangs), who lived at the foot of this mountain. Every day, he chopped wood in a nearby forest. One day, while he was cutting down a pine tree, some dark clouds suddenly hovered above him, and the sunshine disappeared. He raised his head and wondered whether it was going to rain. However, it was an old monster who had caused the sun to disappear. He was flying in the air and holding a beautiful girl under his arm. They were surrounded by ominous dark air. The young man shouted, waved a pole, and managed to hit the monster a few times. Consequently, the monster groaned and flew away. Only his blood was left on the rocks of the cliff.

Next morning, Wang Er went to town to sell the pine wood. He heard people everywhere talking about the princess who had been captured by a monster. The emperor sent out his guards in all directions to find her, but they all failed. Eventually, the emperor announced that whoever found the princess could marry her.

When Wang Er heard the announcement, he scratched his head and thought, "Maybe I can find the princess."

So, he put down his pole and ran to the palace, where he announced that he could find the princess. The guards then took him to the emperor, who asked, "Are you sure that you can find her?"

"Yes, I can," said Wang Er.

"What do you need?"

"I need twenty groups of soldiers and horses, five hundred fat pigs, one sharp ax, one basket with a golden bell tied to it, a rope nine hundred feet long, and a sedan to carry the princess."

The emperor gave him everything he desired.

As soon as Wang Er was satisfied, he went to the place where he had chopped down the pine tree the day before. Once there, he traced the monster's blood to a very remote place—a dark forest near a cliff. It was very dark around the cliff edge where he was. He had no idea how high the cliff was, but guessed it was the entrance to the monster's cave because that was where the traces of blood disappeared. Since Wang Er knew it was the monster's cave, he tied the rope to a fat pig and slowly let it drop down until it was about forty or fifty feet into the cave. A moment later, he pulled up the rope, and there was only blood at the end of the rope. He then lowered several hundred pigs like that until he pulled up the rope and found that the pig was still screaming. Now Wang Er knew it was time to go down into the cave and asked the soldiers, "Who will dare to go down with me?"

All the soldiers were scared, and no one stood up. They just looked at each other. So, Wang Er said, "Since none of you will go down, I will."

He tied one end of the rope to the basket and sat down in it holding an ax.

"Let me down," he commanded. "When you hear the bell, pull me up quickly!"

As soon as he reached the bottom of the cave, he got out of the basket. It was dark all around, but it gradually became bright. Beneath his feet, he saw little monsters everywhere with full bellies and unable to move around. Perhaps they all had eaten too many fat pigs. Therefore, Wang Er killed them with his ax, one by one. When he walked toward the inside of the cave, there were rooms and pavilions. One girl was sitting in the middle of the courtyard. Tears were streaming down her cheeks while she washed some bloody clothes. He recognized the princess right away and was very excited. When the princess noticed him, she asked, "How did you get here, young man?"

"I've come to rescue you," he responded. "Where is the old monster?"

Upon hearing this, the princess stopped weeping and said, "The old monster is in the back room. He is on the bed screaming because someone smashed his head, and he has a bad headache. These bloody clothes are his."

"Well then, you must go and tell him to close his eyes tight because you are going to put some medicine powder on his head. As soon as you do this, I'll kill him."

The princess went to the back room and heard the monster screaming without stopping. So, she pretended to comfort him and said, "Do you still have a headache? I have some good medicine powder. If I put it on your wound, your pain will disappear. But you must close your eyes tight. Otherwise, the medicine will not work."

When the monster closed his eyes, the princess grabbed some dirt from the ground, spread it on his head, and said, "The tighter you close your eyes, the better the medicine works."

Just then, Wang Er sneaked into the room, raised his ax, and chopped off the monster's head. Afterward, he kicked the head away. The princess saw the head rolling toward her, and the monster's body was also moving forward. As the head and the body were about to connect, she shouted to Wang Er, and he chopped the monster's head and body ten times before they stopped moving. Now the monster was clearly dead, and Wang Er was relieved. He turned and gazed at the princess's ivory face and held her hands tight.

"The emperor said that if I rescued you, I could become your husband. Let's leave this place and visit him as soon as possible."

The princess felt shy and followed him to the basket. She wanted Wang Er to climb into the basket and go up first, but he insisted that she should go up first. Finally, the princess got into the basket, and just as Wang Er was about to shake the bell, the princess cried out, "Wait!"

She took off the golden pin from her hair and hit it against a rock. The golden pin broke into two halves, and she gave one half to Wang Er.

"You keep it," she said. "When we meet again, this will be evidence of your courage."

Wang Er put the half of the pin away carefully and then shook the bell very hard. The princess was then pulled up to the top of the cliff. Now Wang Er waited for the basket to come down. However, suddenly, rocks and dirt began to fall from the top. He was scared and ran farther inside the cave. When the noise stopped, the cave entrance was blocked.

There were a lot of things to eat down there in the cave, like pig, cow, and other kinds of meat. Wang Er filled his stomach full and lay on the monster's bed. As he was wondering what his next step should be, he suddenly saw an eel-like fish nailed to the wall. He felt pity for the fish because he felt just like it, stuck in the cave. He then walked up to the fish and pulled out the nail. The fish fell to the ground and then, with a twist, turned into a handsome young man. He smiled at Wang Er and said, "Thank you very much for saving me. I am the third prince of the Dragon King. A few days ago, I came to the cave to play and unfortunately was caught by the monster, who nailed me to the wall. There is a path leading to the sea, and if you follow me to the crystal palace, I'll make sure you reach the shore."

The prince asked Wang Er to close his eyes and lean on his shoulder. Within seconds, Wang Er opened his eyes and saw shining crystals all around him. He felt cold. He saw pearls and gems piled in the corners of the room. Along with mounds of gold sand, there were flocks of crystal silver noodlefish moving from side to side and chasing the jade green shrimps. Despite this marvelous scene, he began to think about the princess and could not appreciate such marvels. So, he begged the prince to send him from the sea to the land. Then, the grateful prince granted his request and carried him to the seashore, where he gave him a Water Propelling Pearl and said, "When you are hungry, it will give you whatever you want to eat."

Wang Er accepted the pearl and began the return journey to his homeland. Whenever he was hungry, he asked the pearl for food. About a month later, he came to a town and heard people saying, "After the princess was found and brought back to the king, she became ill, and unfortunately, the doctors could not diagnose her illness."

Upon hearing this, Wang Er went to the emperor and said, "I can cure the princess."

Since so much time had passed, the emperor could no longer recognize him.

"Are you really sure you can cure her?"

"Do you think I would dare to tell lies to the emperor?"

The emperor then asked a maid to lead him to the princess's pavilion, where she was in feeble condition and sitting in her bed. She seemed to know him one moment, and then not to know him the next. Therefore, Wang Er took out the golden pin and put it next to her. Then she took out her half, and suddenly she came alive and sat up. Her illness disappeared.

You may wonder what led the princess to have this strange illness. It turned out that when she was pulled from the cave, the soldiers immediately pushed her into the sedan and ran back to the palace. She had no idea that the cave had been destroyed. After they had returned to the palace, each one of the soldiers said that he had rescued the princess. When the princess asked for the evidence, none could present it or say anything. She longed for the man who had saved her life. Why hadn't he arrived? She waited one whole day, but he did not appear. She waited another day, but he still did not appear. That was when she became ill. Now Wang Er showed the evidence, and she was extremely delighted. Her heart was full of joy.

They immediately told the whole story to the emperor. The emperor was so angry at the soldiers that he ordered all of them to be killed. Then Wang Er and the princess lived together happily ever after.

3 ■ The Fisherman's Lover

Once there was a notoriously vicious governor who ruled the Hong-tong County. Nobody applied for an official position in that county because of him. All those officials who did work there became scared to death or fell sick. Even if an official there did not become sick, monsters would devour him.

Now, there was a young man whose family name was Wang, but who was nicknamed Bull Demon Head. He wanted to become an official in that county because he did not believe in ghosts or demons. So, he set his heart on learning how to become an official. A few years later, he took the Civil Service Examination. Fortunately, he passed the exam, even though it was the first time that he had taken it. He was then appointed to be the new governor of Hongtong County as a replacement for the former one. His family did not want him to take the position, but he insisted on going there.

Without delaying one minute, he hired some assistants and set off toward Hongtong. They walked for a whole day and arrived at a big inn at dusk. After they checked in, put down their bags, and ate some dinner, they all went to bed. Bull Demon Head stayed in a single room, while his assistants stayed in another larger room. Soon they all fell asleep. Bull Demon Head started dreaming, but, suddenly, he heard a voice calling from outside the window, "Magistrate Wang! Magistrate Wang!"

Bull Demon Head heard the shout and called to his assistants, "Go and search outside my window, and find out who's out there."

The assistants went into the yard holding lanterns and spears in their hands. They searched for a while but found nothing.

"Ok, you all go back to sleep," Bull Demon Head said.

But just as they fell sleep, they heard: "Magistrate Wang! Magistrate Wang!"

Bull Demon Head sat up and called for his assistants yet again.

"Go and search the yard again! Pick up anything in the yard, whether it is a piece of broken brick, tile, cloth, or bone. Collect everything! I must examine whatever you find so that I can understand what is happening here."

All the assistants went out to the yard again and searched for a long time. Yet, they found nothing but a small piece of rotten bone, which they showed to Bull Demon Head.

"Magistrate Wang! There is nothing in the yard but this piece of rotten bone!"

"Give it to me so I can examine it," said Bull Demon Head.

When they presented the bone to him, Magistrate Wang looked at it and said, "All of you, go back to sleep. I shall wrap it in the bag and put it beneath my pillow to find out what it may say."

The assistants all went back to sleep.

After a little while, Magistrate Wang pretended to be asleep. Then he heard the bone saying, "Magistrate Wang! On your way to your office, you must pay a visit to Magistrate Liu. Once you are there, don't accept anything from him except the nine-fold screen. This screen is a treasure. With it, you won't have to be afraid of anything in your office. But you must also take me along as well!"

At daybreak, Magistrate Wang asked the innkeeper to bring in a water basin to wash his face. He drank some tea and ate some breakfast. Then he led his retinue on their journey.

They walked for a whole day until they arrived at Magistrate Liu's courtyard. Magistrate Liu treated Magistrate Wang with wine and food. After eating and drinking, they were about to leave, when

Magistrate Wang said to Magistrate Liu, "May I ask for one thing from you?"

"Whatever you would like," replied Magistrate Liu.

"Nothing else but your nine-fold screen."

Magistrate Liu then sent his housemaids to find it, but they returned and said, "There is no such a thing as a nine-fold screen."

"I am sure you have it. Please search for it more carefully again," said Magistrate Wang.

After a while, they indeed found a very old and ragged nine-fold screen in a small room, but the painting on it was very good. Magistrate Liu gave it to Magistrate Wang without any hesitation. Magistrate Wang wrapped it inside his bag and then bid Magistrate Liu farewell. As they were approaching Hongtong County, they met a group of local men and women. They were all rabbit spirits. The spirits blocked the road, and shouted at them, "Injustice! Injustice!"

Magistrate Wang recognized them as nonhuman and said, "How can you suffer injustice! You are ghosts!"

He ordered his assistants to kill them all, and once they carried out his order, he shouted, "Let's go!"

Soon they reached the entrance to the mansion for county governor. However, the spirits all returned and started a riot. As long as he had the nine-fold screen, Magistrate Wang was not afraid of them. He ordered his assistants to kill them one by one. As they were killing all the spirits, one spirit flew away. It was a doe spirit. It turned into a young wife and escaped. She walked to a riverbank and met a fisherman, and said, "Help me, please! Help me, please!"

"You must have had a quarrel with your husband at home. Let me bring you back home," said the fisherman.

"No, no. Please don't. If you bring me home, I shall lose my life."

"Then how can I help you?"

"Please bring me to your home. That will save me!"

"Certainly," said the fisherman.

He then brought her to his home, where he told his mother everything. In response, his mother said, "She is a woman. It is not very convenient for her to stay in our house. It is better to send her to someone else's home."

The doe spirit cried and even called the old lady "Mother," and said, "Please don't send me back home. I will lose my life if I go back!"

The old lady thought, indeed, how could we allow such a lovely person die? She then agreed to keep her at her home. After a couple of days, the young woman said secretively to the fisherman, "We are now living together, but it is not very convenient in the long run. How about talking to your mother and asking her to let us be husband and wife."

Indeed! The fisherman actually had already had that idea, but he didn't want to offend her by mentioning it first. Now, after their discussion, he was certainly delighted and seized the chance. He then talked to his mother. The old lady was also very happy about it. Consequently, they cleaned up a room, and the couple were married.

The wife was indescribably beautiful, and now that they lived together, the fisherman was exceedingly happy and became totally obsessed with her beauty. He even stopped going out of the house, although the whole family had to live on his fishing. His wife then said, "You have not gone fishing for a long time. What else can we eat? Let me draw a picture of me, and you can take it with you while fishing. Isn't that the same as if we were together?"

"Indeed," said the fisherman.

She then drew a picture of herself that resembled her exact looks. It made the fisherman very happy. So, he took the picture and went out fishing, and when he got to the riverbank, he found a tree branch and hung the picture on it so that he could see her in the picture. This way he could fish while watching her.

Suddenly, there was a gust of wind from the southwest, and the wind blew away the picture. The picture flew back and forth and finally fell into Bull Demon Head's courtyard. When he saw it, he said, "Isn't this the woman who escaped when I first took office?"

He then sent people to search for her and announced that if they did not find her, they would all be killed. Yet, even after he killed many people, there was not a trace of her to be found. The task then fell on the shoulders of an old man who was already in his eighties and said, "How can an old man like me find her?"

"What? Then I will kill you right here!" Bull Demon Head shouted with anger.

"All right, if I can, I shall find her," the old man trembled.

He left the court and went back home, where he lay down in bed without a word. His wife asked, "How come you are staying at home today like this, so forlorn?"

The old man then told her the whole story, and she replied, "How could this be so difficult? Let's figure out a way."

She then went out to the street and found a fortuneteller.

"Mister, tell us a fortune," she asked.

"What?"

"Finding a person."

The blind fortuneteller used his fingers and calculated until he said, "Go southwestward!"

They paid him for the telling and then began walking southwestward.

As they looked around along the way southwestward, they reached a river and saw a fisherman. They then found that there was a picture next to the fisherman. They secretly took out their picture from the old man's chest and compared the two. Immediately, they saw that the picture was the same as theirs. Exactly the same! They looked around and found only one path to the fisherman's home. Therefore, they followed the path, and soon arrived at the house. Once there, they peeked inside the yard above the wall, and saw a woman sprinkling water. It was exactly the woman in the picture!

Soon after, they quickly ran back to Magistrate Wang and reported what they saw. Bull Demon Head was thrilled and immediately summoned his men to mount their horses. He also took his nine-fold screen with him. When they got to the fisherman's house, they surrounded it, and arrested the woman by tying her up. The fisherman heard the noise from afar and ran back home. Upon seeing his wife tied up, he cried and cursed, but the soldiers whipped him.

Bull Demon Head took her back to the court and executed her immediately. From then on, the county never experienced any bad spirits or ghosts.

4 ■ The Silkworm

Once upon a time, there was a military officer who had to bid farewell to his family to participate in a battle on the remote frontier. Besides his wife, he also had a young daughter and a horse.

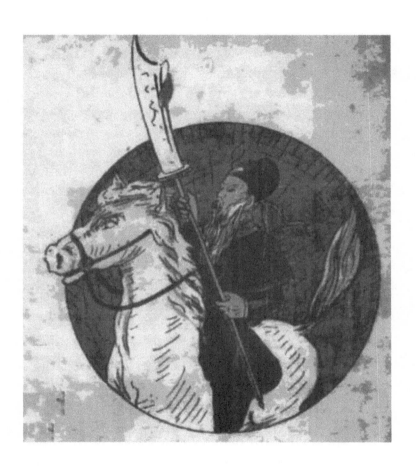

The horse had helped him to achieve many awards in previous battles, and he had decided not to take the horse to any more battles, but to feed the horse the best food.

He left home for a long time without sending word back to his wife and daughter. As a result, they were very worried about him. So, they visited many fortunetellers and tried different ways to discover news about him. Finally, his wife was so worried that she declared: if anyone could bring her husband back home, no matter who it might be, he would be allowed to marry her daughter.

Indeed, many men responded to the announcement, but none of them was successful. After a while, everyone nearby learned about the declaration and kept spreading the word. Since the officer was well known, many young men wanted to be his son-in-law. Finally, the horse also heard about it.

Indeed, when the horse learned about the declaration, he jumped and neighed hysterically, and even stopped eating and drinking. The groom had no idea why he was doing this, but reported everything to his master's wife. When she got to the stable, the horse neighed and jumped even more severely, as if saying that he could find the master. However, she did not understand it. She thought the horse had become tired of living in the stable like a prisoner. She then asked the groom to let the horse go free, and as soon as he was released, he galloped away. For days, no one knew where he went. But when he finally returned, he had his master on his back.

Now, the family had celebrated the reunion and provided greater care for the horse. In particular, they asked the groom to pay special attention to him. But no matter how well the groom treated the horse, he seemed unhappy about everything, restlessly jumping and neighing. Whenever he saw the girl whom he had deserved to marry, he jumped and neighed even harder, as if wanting to kiss her and make love to her.

Later, the master began to notice and was very distressed. There were moments he thought they should keep the promise and wed their daughter to the horse, but eventually he decided to break the promise because the horse had a low status. After he honestly told this to the horse, the horse jumped and neighed very hard as if wanting to die. The master then got angry and killed the horse.

They removed the horse's skin and hung it on the wall of the yard. One day, the girl, who had been promised to the horse, passed by the wall, and all at once, a strange gust of wind arrived, and the horseskin flapped, quickly wrapping up the girl. So, they together became the first silkworm cocoon.

5 ■ On the Celestial Riverbank

At the foot of a wild mountain, there once lived a young man. No one knew his name. His family owned a cow that he always tended, so the people nearby called him Cow Boy.

One summer, the grass on the ground was covered with a layer of thick white fog, and nothing could be seen even from ten feet away. At that time, the old cow was grazing out on the field of grass, and all of a sudden, it turned to Cow Boy and said, "Master, in the river south of this field of grass, there are seven fairies, and they are bathing there. Therefore, I suggest that you sneak to the riverbank, fetch a set of clothes with gems, and hide it. Then one of the fairies will become your wife."

At these words, Cow Boy rushed to the riverbank, and indeed, saw seven fairies in the foggy mist. Then he noticed seven sets of clothes lined with gems on the bank. Without thinking, he uttered a loud shout, grabbed one set of clothes, and ran away. The fairies were very shy and quickly covered themselves with their clothes. Then, they flew up into the sky, except one fairy. Her name was Weaving Girl. She remained there stark naked and blushed with anxiety. She tried to chase Cow Boy and begged him to return her clothes. However, he refused and ran all the way home. The fairy followed him, but Cow Boy hid her clothes before she noticed. Consequently, she could not fly up to the clouds with her celestial clothes. She had to put on some human clothes and became Cow Boy's wife. She enjoyed weaving when she was in the celestial palace, and she even carried her weaving stick with her when she came down to the earth. So, she was somewhat content.

Now that Cow Boy had a wife, he did not want to herd the old cow any more. He let the cow go to the field of grass by itself. Before long, the cow got so sick that it just slept on a pile of grass. When Cow Boy saw the poor cow, he stroked its back and felt extremely sad. The cow raised its head and said, "Master, I am dying. After I die, you are to remove my skin and wrap a lump of yellow sand in it as a bag. Then untie the rope around my neck and tie up the bag. You should carry it on your shoulders every day. When you get in any trouble, it will help you."

After these words, the cow died. Cow Boy thought of the days he had spent with the cow and their shared hardships. Indeed, he could not help but weep, and in tears, he did what the cow told him to do.

Two or three years passed. Weaving Girl gave birth to a daughter and a son. During this time, she often asked Cow Boy where he had hidden her celestial clothes, but he always tried to talk about something else. Now she again asked him and said, "Where did you hide my celestial clothes? Now that you and I have a daughter and son, how would I want to leave?"

Cow Boy thought she was right and replied with smiles, "I am afraid they are rotten now. They are buried underneath the step of stone at the door."

So the fairy ran to the door, lifted the stone, and picked up the clothes. They were still shining. She threw them over her body and then flew up to the clouds. Cow Boy got worried. He grabbed the two children and wanted to chase her, but how could they catch her since they could not control the clouds? Cow Boy was so anxious that he accidentally touched the bag on his back, and as he tapped the cowskin bag, the three of them, Cow Boy and the two children, suddenly flew and grabbed hold of the clouds. Immediately, they began to chase Weaving Girl.

When Weaving Girl saw that they were pursuing her, she took off her golden hairpin and drew a line behind her. Immediately, the line became a big river with turbulent waves. Unexpectedly, Cow Boy's cowskin bag leaked some yellow sand that quickly became a dam. They ran across the river along the dam. Weaving Girl saw they were getting closer to her again. Therefore, she took the golden hairpin and drew another big river with turbulent waves. Because all the yellow sand from CowBoy's bag had run out, they could not cross the river. Consequently, he quickly untied the bag and threw one end of the rope to the east, and it just caught Weaving Girl's neck. She took out her weaving stick and threw it at him, but he swatted it away.

As they were struggling and fighting each other, a white-bearded immortal appeared from the edge of the sky. He was holding a cane, and said to them, "I came here at the order of the Celestial Emperor to solve your dispute. Weaving Girl, from now on, you are to stay on the east side of the river. Cow Boy, from now on, you stay on the west side of the river. Since your fortune has not run to an end, you can meet with Weaving Girl only on the night of the seventh day of the seventh month every year."

It was impossible for them not to heed the words of the Celestial Emperor. So, now if you see lots of stars on autumn nights, lift your head, and you will see a celestial river across the sky. This celestial river was drawn by Weaving Girl's golden hairpin. She and Cow Boy live on each side of the river and are the blinking bright stars. The small star next to Weaving Girl is the weaving spindle. The small stars around Cow Boy are their daughter and son and the weaving stick.

On the day after Cow Boy stops shining, he leaves a bowl for Weaving Girl to wash. During the night, they meet, and she finishes washing the bowl just at the time that the day breaks. It is said that on the seventh day of the seventh month each year, if there is no rain, it is an auspicious sign. But if there is rain, the raindrops are the tears from their eyes.

6 ■ The Flute Player

Once there was a young man named Abo (Protected Boy). He lived a humble life with his mother because he had lost his father many years earlier. Even though their life was full of hardship, Abo did not want to find a job. He played his bamboo flute (*xiao*) all the time. His flute was made of bamboo, but it sounded so touching when he played that those who passed by his home would stop to listen. Indeed, those people who were working would stand up; those who were crying would forget their sorrow; those who were angry would calm down; and sometimes even the birds would stop flying and the fish would stop swimming.

Abo was so passionate about his flute that he would rather not eat than stop playing. To him, the flute was more important and precious than food or even his own life. Whenever his mother said, "If you play the flute again, you will not be allowed to eat," his answer would always be: "The flute is my meal, and I'd rather play the flute."

His obsession with the flute made his mother very angry, and one day she said to him: "Since you don't want to find a job and make a living, I want you to leave this house right away."

So, Abo left his home, and while he was walking to the seashore, he thought that the sea, which roared every day, might become his good friend. He then sat on the seashore facing the sea and began to play the flute along with roaring of the sea waves. In fact, his flute sounded so graceful and lively that it wakened the Sea Dragon King, who then sent a crab general to find out who was playing the flute so beautifully.

"When you see him, invite him here," the Sea Dragon King said.

The crab general took the order and rushed to the seashore, where he saw Abo sitting there playing the flute. Therefore, he opened a water path to reach him and walked over to him.

"My master would like to meet with you," he said.

"Who is your master?" asked Abo.

"The Sea Dragon King."

"What does he want from me?" Abo asked again.

"To play the flute. He heard you play and really praised you," answered the crab general.

At these words, Abo followed the crab general, who opened a water path and led him to the king.

The palace of the Sea Dragon King was made of crystals, and the chairs and tables were made of coral. Everything was so shiny and glittering that Abo could hardly open his eyes. When the Sea Dragon King saw Abo, he welcomed him and said, "You play the flute very well. I purposely invited you to play one song for me."

"Of course," said Abo.

He sat on a chair of red coral and began to play a graceful melody. The king listened and was very attentive. Then the king asked for one more, and then one after another. Therefore, Abo played until late into the night. The Sea Dragon King was so pleased that he wanted his daughter to wed Abo. So, Abo stayed there.

Without noticing the time, Abo had already lived in the palace for three years. One day, he suddenly missed his home and his mother. He wanted to return home immediately and told all this to the princess. Well, the princess was very considerate and thought that since he missed his mother so much, she should not force him to stay.

"If my father wants to give you anything when you leave," she said, "you are just to take the All-Promise Box and the All-Wish Stick."

So, the princess went to her father with Abo and pleaded for him. The king, too, was sympathetic and permitted Abo to leave because he missed his mother so much.

"Since you are leaving," the King said, "I would like to give you some jewels. What do you want?"

"I don't want anything except the All-Promise Box and the All-Wish Stick," said Abo.

The king then gave those to him and asked the crab general to lead him to his home. Soon thereafter, they came out of the water path and back to the seashore where Abo used to play the flute. He stood at the seashore for a little while and then walked toward his home. When he got home, his mother was extremely happy.

"Mother," he said, "I must tell you that we don't have to worry about food anymore. We have special gifts now."

He then tested his gifts and asked something from the All-Promise Box and then tapped the box with the All-Wish Stick. Indeed, whenever he touched the box with the All-Wish Stick he would get what he wanted. Soon he had a big house, a beautiful wife, plentiful food, and clothes for all seasons. In short, he now had everything.

His neighbor saw him getting rich overnight and heard that he had a special gift, so he asked, "May I borrow and use your special gift?"

"Yes, of course," Abo said.

When the neighbor brought the box and the stick to his home, he kept hitting the box with the stick, but he received nothing. Therefore, he became so angry that he threw them on the ground, and said, "I don't want these things anymore!"

Strangely enough, as he uttered those words, the All-Promise Box and the All-Wish Stick disappeared.

7 ■ The Pheasant Feather Cloak

Once there was a blacksmith, who happened one day to see the daughter of a rich man, and he decided he would marry her. Therefore, he said to his mother, "I want to marry the rich man's daughter."

"What? Are you crazy? How can a rich man's daughter be willing to marry you?" the mother responded.

"She must become my wife," the blacksmith insisted.

The next morning, the blacksmith got up very early, went to the rich man, and said, "Your daughter is extremely beautiful. Would you let her marry me?"

"Of course, yes!" the rich man said without hesitation. "But, you must do one thing for me first. If you can manage to do this chore, then I'll let my daughter marry you."

Then, the rich man invited him into a different room. He lifted a big bucket of rapeseeds and sesame seeds and poured them on a table. Then he asked the blacksmith to separate them, and added, "Tomorrow I shall come to see whether you have performed this task."

The blacksmith sat there motionlessly and thought to himself, "This is really difficult! But even if I want to leave now, it is not easy to get out."

He couldn't think of a way to do it, and he was to blame for not starting to separate the seeds right away. Even by the evening, he had not begun working. In fact, he became very tired, and so he buried his head on the table, and fell asleep.

Just at this time, a gust of wind blew into the room through the window. Along with the wind, a white tiger jumped into the room. He put his nose on the table and puffed three times. The rapeseeds and sesame seeds seemed to have legs, ran away, and separated. The white tiger then disappeared.

In the morning, the blacksmith woke up and saw that all the rapeseeds and sesame seeds had been separated. He was thrilled and jumped for joy. Soon, the rich man opened the door and entered. He was shocked by the miraculous scene. He thought that the blacksmith had to have been helped by a magic power. Consequently, he let the blacksmith marry his daughter.

After the blacksmith married the rich man's daughter, he refused to work outside the house. Therefore, one day his wife asked him, "Why don't you go out to work?"

"I can't stay away from you. You are really too beautiful!"

"If you go to work, I shall paint a picture of me so that you can see me all the time," she responded.

So, the blacksmith carried his wife's picture to work. He would look at the picture as he walked, and he would also look at the picture while sharpening knives and scissors. At one time, as he sat down and got ready to sharpen a pair of scissors for a family, there was a sudden gust of wind, and it blew the picture away to the king's garden. The king picked it up and fell in love with the picture.

"Is there really such a beautiful woman as the one in this picture?" he asked himself.

He then sent his ministers all over his realm to find this lady. When, indeed, they found her, the king, with his guards, went to the blacksmith's house. Immediately, the blacksmith knew that the king would take away his wife, and he cried with great sorrow. However, his wife said to him, "Don't be sad. I will always be your wife. Remember, when a southeast wind arrives next month, you are to wear a pheasant feather cloak and go to the king's castle to do your sharpening work."

Then the king took the blacksmith's wife to the king's castle. She never smiled even once after she arrived at the castle. The king tried all sorts of ways to make her smile, but never succeeded.

One day, a gust of the southeast wind arrived while the king and the blacksmith's wife were drinking wine in the garden. Suddenly, they heard, "Knives to sharpen! Scissors to sharpen!"

She began laughing, and the king was delighted.

"What made you laugh at this?" he asked.

"Listen! That sound is so interesting!" she remarked.

"You like this sound? I'll have him sent in," said the King.

Dressed in pheasant feather cloak, the blacksmith entered, and with each step he took, she laughed even harder.

"Why do you laugh so hard?" the king asked.

"Just look! His feather cloak is so beautiful!" she remarked.

"If you like his cloak, then I shall wear it," said the king.

The blacksmith took off his pheasant cloak, and the king put it on. Then the blacksmith's wife stepped forward and stabbed the king to death. Now the blacksmith took his place and became king.

8 ■ The Sea Dragon King

Once there was a young fisherman who dove into a deep river to catch some fish. When he came to a cave at the bottom of the river, it turned out to be the gate of the palace of the Sea Dragon King. Just then, two princesses changed into two big fish and began playing at the gate. The fisherman caught them and brought them to the market to sell, but nobody wanted to buy such big fish.

When the Sea Dragon King learned about this, he sent his night guards to catch the fisherman and bring him to the palace so he could kill him. However, to the Sea Dragon King's surprise, one of the princesses fell in love with the fisherman and asked her father to make the fisherman her husband. The Sea Dragon King then released him and made him the princess's husband.

One day, the Sea Dragon King demanded that the fisherman was to catch a squid of one pound and four ounces with a three-foot bucket within one day. However, the fisherman had no way of doing this, and so he returned home crying.

"Why are you weeping?" the princess asked.

"The Sea Dragon King wanted me to catch a squid weighing one pound and four ounces with a three-foot bucket, and I must bring it to him within one day," he said. "But there aren't many squid that heavy!"

The princess then changed into a squid of one pound and four ounces in a three-foot bucket. Then the fisherman brought the squid to the king.

The king then demanded that he catch a turtle weighing one pound and four ounces with a three-foot bucket. Since he had no idea of how to catch it, he returned home crying.

The princess asked him again, "Why are you weeping?"

"The Sea Dragon King wants me to catch a turtle weighing one pound and four ounces with a three-foot bucket," he said. "But there aren't many turtles that big!" he said.

The princess then changed herself into a turtle weighing one pound and four ounces in a three-foot bucket. Then the fisherman brought the turtle to the king.

In response, the king demanded that he catch a fish weighing one pound and four ounces with a three-foot bucket. However, he had no clue how to catch it and he returned home crying.

"Why are you weeping?" asked the princess.

"The Sea Dragon King wants me to catch a fish weighing one pound and four ounces with a three-foot bucket," he said. "However, there aren't many fish that weigh just that much!"

The princess changed into a fish weighing one pound and four ounces in a three-foot bucket, and the fisherman brought the fish to the king.

When the king saw that he had completed all the tasks and he did not have any harder tasks for the fisherman, he sent a demonic monster to guard the gate so that the fisherman could not get out. The fisherman became worried and knelt down to beg the demon to let him escape, but the demon ignored him.

The princess waited at home for a long time, but she did not see her husband return. She went looking for him. When she came to the palace gate and saw a demonic monster guarding the gate and her husband kneeling down and begging him, she captured the monster and set her husband free so that he could go home with her. They kept the demonic monster at home and fed it with burning charcoal every day.

Later, the Sea Dragon King devoured the demonic monster.

9 ■ The Celestial Fairy

In ancient times, there was a young man named Zhang San (third son of the Zhangs). One day, he was gathering waterweeds along the river. Suddenly, an old moose ran to him and cried, "Uncle, Uncle! Save me! A hunter is after me! Please, let me hide in the pile of grass. When he gets here, just tell him that I ran to the other side of the mountain."

"The grass pile is very small. There's not even enough there to cook for a meal. You are so big. How can you hide there?" Zhang San replied.

"I can change myself into a small thing," the old moose said and rolled on the ground. Then he changed himself into a small rabbit and squeezed into the pile.

Soon a hunter appeared. He was blowing a bamboo whistle and was accompanied by his big yellow dog. "Uncle, Uncle! Did you see an old moose running by this place?" he asked Zhang San.

"I saw it running and fleeing to the other side of the mountain," Zhang San said.

At these words, the hunter rushed to the other side of the mountain. After the hunter left, the old moose came out of the grass pile. He now changed himself into an old man and thanked Zhang San, "Uncle, Uncle! Thank you so much for saving my life. Please let me take you to visit my house."

Zhang San did not want to go, but was nevertheless dragged away by the old man. The two of them walked for half a mile and arrived at the foot of a mountain. There was a path leading to the middle of the mountain with old trees and cliffs along the two sides blocking the light from the sky. Then they arrived at a cave covered by a pile of morning glory vines. The cave door was tightly closed. The old man stretched out his hairy hand and tapped twice on the door. Then a group of small moose ran over and opened the door.

"Grandpa, Grandpa, who is that behind you?" the small moose asked.

"This is your Second Grandpa," said the old moose.

All of the small moose were happy to meet their Second Grandpa. The old moose invited Zhang San to sit in a big hall with red walls. He took out a set of precious clothes and asked him to put them on. Soon, the small moose prepared a table of wine and hot dishes. Zhang San had never tasted these dishes before.

After eating, he wanted to return home and said that his mother must be starving to death. "Don't worry. Where is your home?" the old moose said.

"A small hut in the front of the mountain," he replied.

"I'll have my children bring ten bags of rice to her and build a big house for you. You just stay here without worrying about those things," the old moose said.

Three or four days quickly passed. By then, Zhang San had eaten a lot of meat and fish, and he insisted on going home to see his mother. As he was about to set off, the old moose asked him whether he had a wife.

"No. I don't have a wife," he replied.

"There is a garden in my backyard," the old moose said. "There are eight fairy ladies taking a bath in the pond. Their clothes are hung on the trees near the pond. You are to go and grab a set of clothes and run home. One of the fairies will follow you, and she will naturally become your wife."

Zhang San ran to the backyard garden and saw endless old trees. As he walked, the path became narrower and narrower and was sheltered by tree branches. In order to move forward, he had to turn sideways. Then he saw a pond toward the north shining like a mirror. He could vaguely see a few girls bathing in the pond. On the flower trees near the pond, there were some colorful clothes. He sneaked to the flower tree, grabbed a set of clothes, turned around, and ran away. He ran all the way home and saw there were big houses with tile roofs surrounding his old hut. He knew that they were built by the small moose and was so excited that he ran to his mother and shouted, "Mother! Your son is back!"

His mother was old and had poor vision. The night that he had been dragged away by the old moose she had suffered from hunger and had rolled back and forth and cried like a ghost. The small moose had carried ten bags of rice over and had quietly built the houses surrounding the hut, and then had returned to their cave. The old woman had suffered from hunger until the next morning and complained about her son not coming back home. She then remembered they had one cabbage. She opened the door, but saw that there were walls all around. "How come all the paths are blocked by ghosts even at daytime?" she said to herself. She rubbed her eyes and looked around. Those were big tile-roof houses. She searched her way to the nearest room, and there was a lot of rice. She made a pot of porridge in a hurry, and ate it. She lived in confusion for three or four days, and thought she was dreaming all the time.

On that day, when her son returned home, she was wondering what had happened. She heard her son shouting in front of her. She saw her son in a shining robe, carrying some perfumed clothes. Then, a girl entered the yard and asked her son to return the clothes. The mother felt very peculiar and kept blinking her eyes, looking at her son with amazement. Zhang San said to his mother, "Mother, don't be surprised. The night I did not come home, I saved the life of an old moose. He then sent his children to bring over ten bags of rice and to build the houses. During that time, he kept me in his cave for a few days. When I was ready to return, he arranged a marriage for me. She is a fairy from the sky," he said while pointing at the fairy. "Mother! Look at this beautiful girl. She is now your daughter-in-law!"

His mother was so happy that her mouth dropped wide open for a while. Then she jumped with joy. The fairy who had chased Zhang San was called Hua Gu, meaning that she was a magnificently beautiful fairy. Her home was in the deep mountains in the north. She begged Zhang San to return her clothes, but he always refused. He secretly buried the clothes under a flower tree.

Since Hua Gu was unable to get her celestial clothes back on her body, she could not ride on the clouds. She was very shy and had no choice but to become his wife. Two years later, they had a baby who was both white and chubby.

One cloudy day, it began drizzling. Zhang San suddenly remembered to visit the old moose. As he was about to leave, Hua Gu held him by the hands and said, "Where on earth did you hide my clothes? I've been with you for years and now we have our baby. Why would I be willing to leave you?"

He was anxious to leave, but he couldn't unless he answered her. Moreover, what Hua Gu said made good sense. She wouldn't leave even if he returned her clothes. So, he told her the truth, "They are buried underneath the flower tree east of the house."

Hearing these words, Hua Gu let him go, and when he arrived at the old moose's cave, the old moose said, "What are you doing here? Hua Gu took the baby and left. How could she not leave once she got her clothes?"

Zhang San looked at the old moose, and wanted to cry.

"Don't cry," the old moose said. "I'll give you a small bottle. If you hold it in your mouth, you won't be hungry for a hundred days. Now you are to head straight north for seven days and seven nights. Then you will find your wife."

He took the bottle and went back home to bid farewell to his mother. On the same day, he put the small bottle in his mouth and set off on the lonely journey. He walked three days and then came to a big river blocking his way. There was no boat nor bridge. How could he cross it?

On the bank across the river, there was a small hut. An old woman was sitting at the door, singing while weaving. Zhang San greeted her, "Grandma! How can I cross the river?"

The old woman held a thread on her left hand and threw the spindle across the river to the south bank with her right hand. Thus, there was a long thread meandering across the river.

"You can walk on this thread and cross the river," she said.

He was so anxious to see Hua Gu that he took a deep breath, walked on the thread, and safely crossed the river. Indeed, he walked northward for seven days and seven nights. Then, he arrived at a wild mountain. At the break of day, he saw a child sitting on a rock on top of a cliff. The child looked like his. He walked up to the child, and indeed, it was his child. Once he held the child in his arms, he cried, "Oh, my baby!"

However, he had been walking for seven days and nights and his face was covered with dust, so the baby did not recognize him. He was scared and began crying. Then, Zhang San heard someone walking along the creek. He raised his head and saw Hua Gu walking toward him. She held Zhang San's hands and cried, "You took the trouble to come all the way here. I am so sorry. My mother enjoys tricking people and has numerous goblins around here. When she asks you to eat, please don't eat anything!"

She carried the baby and led Zhang San to a big house. Inside, an old woman was smoking a tobacco pipe. Once she saw them enter, she asked Hua Gu, "Who is this young man?"

"Mother, this is your son-in-law!" Hua Gu replied.

"Oh, my son-in-law," the old woman said quickly in a polite manner. "My good boy, you must be hungry. Let me get you something to eat."

"I am not hungry," he replied.

"Well, then you must be tired after walking such a long way. Why don't you take a rest in the east room?" the old woman said.

Zhang San entered the east room followed by Hua Gu. She took out a green handkerchief and said, "No matter what happens tonight, so long as you keep this handkerchief on your face, you will be all right."

She then left the room. When night came, Zhang San covered his face and fell asleep in bed. Flocks of mosquitos flew in, and they were as big as water buffalos, blinking eyes with fire sparkles inside. The little ones said to the older one, "Let's eat! Let's eat!"

The old one circled over Zhang San's face and said, "Are you blind? Isn't this Hua Gu? She covered her face with this green handkerchief and is sound asleep. If she is bitten awake, how can we tolerate the punishment? Hurry out! Hurry out!"

Consequently, all the goblins flew out one by one. In the morning, the old woman asked the little goblins to collect the human bones in the east room. The little goblins took brooms and went to the east room, but found no bones at all, only one young man who was staring outside. The goblins reported to the old woman, who frowned, and said, "Let him sleep in the west room tonight."

In the evening, Zhang San walked into the west room followed by Hua Gu.

"No matter what happens tonight, so long as you keep this handkerchief on your face, you will be all right," she said, and then left the room.

When night came, Zhang San covered his face and fell asleep in bed. Flocks of black fleas flew into the room, and they were fiercer than wild dogs and as big as water buffalos. The old flea goblin had a red stomach because it had sucked in too much human blood, and its stomach was about to explode. Its eyes were as big as copper bells and were already swollen and blind. It smelled the human, and then shouted at the small flea goblins, "Take me there! Take me there! I want to eat it!"

The little ones leaped to the bed and shouted at the old one, "You are such an old blind flea! Isn't this Hua Gu? She covered her face with this green handkerchief and is sound asleep. If we bite and wake her, how can we tolerate the punishment? Hurry out! Hurry out!"

They then dragged the old blind flea out of the room quietly. In the morning, the old woman asked the small goblins to collect the human bones in the west room. The little goblins took brooms and went into the west room, but found no bones, only a young man (who they had seen in the east room) staring outside. They reported to the old woman, who laughed loudly and said, "He indeed has great courage and talent. Then I'll keep him as my son-in-law."

From then on, Zhang San and Hua Gu lived happily in the wild mountains. However, with regard to Zhang San's mother, I don't have the slightest clue as to what happened to her.

10 ■ The Daughter of the Dragon King of the Sea

Once there were a mother and her son who lived in a hut, wore shabby clothes, and ate very simple meals. Now, the son was about thirteen or fourteen years old and began an apprenticeship with a carpenter. He worked from morning till night and worked according to the agreement "with food but without wages." Consequently, he could not help his mother at all.

After three hard years had passed, he finished the apprenticeship, and his master gave him one silver coin and told him to go back home to see his mother. Now that he had a silver coin in his pocket, he felt extremely happy. Even a millionaire would not perhaps have enjoyed this moment of contentment as the young man did.

"I want to buy a fish to show my filial dedication to my mother," he said. "What a pity that she has never had a taste of fish soup since my father died!"

When he walked out of the master's house, he saw a fisherman coming toward him with a fish basket in his right hand. There was a big, fat carp in the basket. The young man stood there, stared at the fish, and thought, "I remember my mother liked to eat carp fish most. Why not buy it now and bring it to her?"

"How much is your fish?" he asked.

The fisherman saw him in worn clothes, without matching socks and shoes, and thought he certainly wouldn't have enough money to buy the fish. So, he said, "If you can pay me five hundred cents, I will sell it to you."

In fact, the fish was worth more than a silver coin.

"You think I can't afford it?" the young man responded, while taking out his silver coin. "Here! Give me the change!"

Since the fisherman had thought that the young man couldn't afford the fish, he became speechless. Moreover, he could not go back on his offer. Therefore, he sold his big fish at a very low price, and the young man returned home with the fish. When mother and son met, they were so happy that the tears ran down their cheeks. Then he showed his mother the fish he had bought, and said, "Mother, guess how much I paid for it?"

"My good son, I can't see anything. Ever since you left, I worked day and night, and I am now blind."

As he looked at his mother's eyeballs, he saw that they were indeed white, but without any brightness. Although her eyes looked as if nothing had happened to them, she could not see anything. He wept with great sorrow and said, "I'll find the best eye doctor for you!"

"Don't go. I once went to a doctor, and he told me that my eyes had lost light and could never be healed!"

"I don't believe it. I'll find a good doctor. No matter where under the heavens, I will find a good doctor for you," and he ran out of the house even though she tried to hold him back.

So, she had no choice but to let him go. After the young man left, she put the fish in a big water jar and covered the jar with a bucket.

The fish now had water to feel comfortable, but soon would be killed and scaled on the cutting board. The son and his mother did not know that the fish was actually the daughter of the Dragon King of the Sea. When she had been young and naïve, she had gone out alone to play without telling her parents and was then caught by the fisherman. In her grief, she cried out, "Mother . . . come and save me!"

Even though her parents sent all the shrimp soldiers and crab generals to all the big and small rivers, they could not find her. They had no idea that she was now stuck in a water jar!

She waited a while, but no one came to rescue her. Then she had an idea: she imitated the cat and began to cry "meow, meow, meow, . . ." without stopping.

The old woman heard the cat meowing and thought, "It's not easy for my son to get a fish to show his respect for me. So, it's better not to let the cat steal the fish. It's better to kill and cook the fish now."

She then went to the water jar, took away the bucket, and put her hands into the water jar to grab the fish. When the carp realized what was happening, she flexed her tail very hard and splashed the water all over and even hit the old woman's eyes. Amazingly, once the old woman wiped her eyes, they became bright, and she could see things and could even see a needle dropped on the ground.

The old woman was so surprised and happy that she did not want to kill the fish. Therefore, she kept it in the big jar. The fish seemed to know that she would not be killed and became happy in the water, swimming back and forth.

Before long, the son returned and was very angry.

"Mother!" he exclaimed. "It is so annoying. When I went out to the east gate, I saw the eye doctor's sign, and it said he could cure seven times seven, forty-nine types of eye problems, immediately effective! I then went in to ask him to come and examine your eyes. He asked for one silver coin. Since I had already used my silver coin, I said, to him, 'Once you are at my house, I'll pay you even by selling everything in the house.' But he simply pushed me out of his shop, and even scolded me, 'Go and beg for a handout elsewhere. Don't waste my time!'"

"Don't be angry," his mother replied. "My eyes are good now. They are even brighter than they were!"

"What? What happened? Can a hatching hen give birth to a duck with a blink of an eye? Who cured your eyes?"

His mother then told him everything that had happened to her.

"Wonderful! This is a miracle! A fish that cost five hundred cents is better than a doctor who demands one silver coin! Moreover, he might not even cure you! The fish is indeed our benefactor. We should release it. Mother, let's go right now and release it."

The mother and son then took the fish out of the jar, put it in a basket, ran to the seashore, gently put it into the water, and said, "Take care. Be careful in the future. Don't let people catch you anymore. If you are caught again, you may not be released easily by others."

Strangely enough, the fish swam a few feet away, but then turned around, raised her head, looking at them, as if trying to remember their appearances. When the young man saw that she was not willing to swim away, he scolded her, "Go! Stupid. Go quickly! If you stay here, you will be caught by someone else. You wouldn't be happy about that!"

However, the fish still stared at him and did not want to leave.

He said again, "If you want to show your gratitude to me, you can swim three rounds, then I will know what you mean, and you can go."

At these words, the fish indeed swam three rounds and nodded at him. Then she swam to the deep sea and disappeared.

The fish, the incarnation of the daughter of the Dragon King of the Sea, went back to the crystal palace under the sea. Everyone was very happy when she returned home. She told her father what had happened to her, and her father said to her, "Now you must return their favor! You'd better go now, and we can have our reunion three years from now."

"Indeed," the daughter said. "When he released me, I had the same thought." Then, she went to her own room. A moment later, a beautiful girl came out, in her most beautiful and most precious clothes. The other fish spirits all praised her with great admiration.

"Father, I am leaving," she said.

Once she had created a water path and come to the seashore, she walked toward the hut where the young man lived. Only the mother was in the hut. The son had gone to do something away from home. When she walked into the hut and saw the mother weaving, she said, "Mother, what a pity. It is dark now. I can't find a place to stay. Please let me stay here for one night."

When the old woman saw that she was so beautiful and in such precious clothes, she said, "You can indeed stay here, but our hut is small and dirty. How can it be appropriate for you to stay here?"

"I don't mind your small and dirty hut at all. I shall be grateful so long as you keep me for the night," she replied.

The old woman saw that she was honest and let her stay. As they were talking, the son returned. When he saw a beautiful girl sitting inside his hut, his face flushed red and he wanted to step outside. The daughter of the Dragon King of the Sea saw him, and said, "Please come in. There is nothing embarrassing." And then she said to the mother, "Is he your son? He has a blessed face."

"Can you tell fortunes by face-reading, my lady?" asked the mother.

"Yes. I have told fortunes for many people, but have never seen a face as good-looking as his. Old Mother, I have something to say, but I am not sure if you will promise to say yes."

"Please feel free to say anything. If I can, I will definitely say yes," the mother replied.

"I really want to be your daughter-in-law," she said.

Hearing this, the son was so shy that he quickly withdrew from the hut. Then the mother said, "My lady, are you crazy? A family like ours . . . how can you make us accept you!"

"I am serious. The two of you have good hearts and will be blessed to have a good future. I am willing to be your daughter-in-law."

The mother tried to decline, but the daughter insisted. Finally, the mother thought, "Since she is so sincere, it is also good for me to arrange a family for my son."

"However," the mother said, "we only have this hut, how can we let you live here? The bed is not clean enough. How can you sleep on it?"

"Don't worry. Do you have extra unused land?"

"Unused land? There is a big piece of unused land in the backyard. But it is not worth anything."

"That's not the case. Since there is unused land, I can build a house," the daughter said.

The mother thought it was a joke and did not pay much attention to her words. She then took out a clean quilt and a sheet to cover the bed for the newlyweds' first night.

After a little while, the newlyweds went to bed and fell asleep. Then all of a sudden, at midnight, the bride seemed to give an order to someone, "Let the carpenter and the mason be in charge of building a house."

"It's midnight," her husband said. "You'd better sleep now. Are you talking in your sleep?"

The bride did not answer him, but continued saying something like that. At the same time, there seemed to be a great number of people in the backyard, with noises of sawing wood and building bricks. It seemed there were hundreds of people busy building a house.

Before long, the bride said again, "Get the painter to paint everything well." After saying this, she fell asleep.

Strangely enough, the next morning, they looked into the backyard and suddenly saw a very fine house of four rooms that glittered with lots of expensive furniture and decorations inside.

The mother and son were both amazed, and exclaimed, "What? This is indeed a miracle! How can such a big house be built overnight? What a beautiful house! But we did not see any workers!"

They were so excited with the splendid house and thought, "It doesn't matter whether she has magic power or not. We have been so poor, and now can enjoy our fortune."

They then all moved into the new house, where they found many servants and wardrobes in each bedroom with clothes for all the seasons. All three—mother, son, and princess—were very happy. The young carpenter did not even go out to work, but kept company with his wife at home.

Time flew by quickly. Two years passed by. In these two years, the princess gave birth to a son, and the boy had a big head and big ears, just like his father. The young carpenter had a maternal cousin with whom he used to hang out, but in the past two years, the young carpenter did not go to his cousin's house. One day, the two met on the road. The cousin knew that the carpenter had become rich and had a wife as beautiful as a fairy from the heavens. Therefore, he wanted to catch up with his younger cousin and talk about things. He invited him to drink in his house, and the young carpenter agreed.

But when he told his wife that he had agreed to have a drink in his cousin's house, his wife protested and said, "I know for sure that your cousin doesn't have a good heart. So, you are not to go there."

Indeed, the carpenter listened to his wife, and on the day he had agreed to go, he sent a message to tell his cousin that he would not be coming. Next year, during the first month of the New Year, the cousin came and invited the young carpenter again to drink the New Year wine. And now the carpenter's wife said to her husband, "You can go, and since I know that he will want something from you, you can promise him anything he wants."

When the young carpenter arrived at his cousin's house, his cousin prepared a rich banquet. After eating a while, the cousin said to the young carpenter, "I heard that your wife is very beautiful, just like a fairy from the heavens. You are so lucky to have married such a woman!"

The young carpenter humbly replied with some polite words.

"Now I want to have a word with you about your wife," the cousin said, "and it may be offensive to you. So, are you willing to listen?"

"Say anything you want. You know that you can say anything to me."

"Well, it is a shameful thing for me. I admire your wife very much. Therefore, I want to exchange your wife for my wife and concubine. If you kindly agree, I would be forever grateful!"

The young carpenter got so angry after he heard these words that he wanted to curse his cousin to his face, but he remembered what his wife had told him with particular emphasis, and then said, "Perhaps it is possible. But I need to ask her first."

After all, he thought he could not promise such a thing alone.

"Then, that is good. Please go to ask your wife. But I think she will agree because to exchange one woman for two women is an excellent deal."

The young carpenter kept quiet while his cousin was talking. He finished eating and drinking in low spirits, and then left his cousin. After he got home, he sat alone in the house and became even angrier. Then his wife came to him and asked, "How come you are so unhappy? What did your cousin say to you?"

"Damn! I can't tell you. He's a beast!"

"Just tell me. We can talk about it."

"He said he admired your beauty and wanted to give me his wife and a concubine in exchange for you. Do you think this is a reasonable thing?"

"Did you agree?"

"I said that I needed to come and ask you. But how can I say that I agree?"

"You can go now and tell him, yes. Tell him I am willing to exchange so long as he agrees to give you a chest."

"That's impossible! How can I be away from you?"

"Just go and tell him this. And listen to me! I must punish this evil man. Also, I have given birth to a son for you, and I can return to my home now."

"Return to where?"

"Return to my father's palace."

"What? I have never heard you talk about your father. Who is your father? Where is he?"

"Don't ask any more. Just go. You will know later."

Now, her husband listened and obeyed her. As he was about to go, she told him again, "You must ask him to send his wife and concubine over here first. Then send a sedan to fetch me. I can't walk on my own feet to his place. Also, if he agrees to give you a chest, ask only for the small black leather chest in his bedroom, nothing else."

The husband remembered all these words and left.

When he arrived at his cousin's house, his cousin asked, "How was it? Did she agree?"

"She agreed indeed, but she has two conditions: first, you must send your women over first; second, you must give me a chest, and I am the only one to carry it."

When the cousin heard that his sister-in-law had agreed, his heart was full of joy. Then he quickly replied, "That is nothing! I'll do everything she said. Please, go to my room and fetch the chest."

When the young carpenter went to the room, he saw a small black leather chest on top of a pile of big chests.

"That's the one I want," he said.

"Very good. Just take it. When is your wife coming?"

"After your women are sent over, you are to send a sedan to fetch her."

"That's wonderful. Now I'll go to hire a sedan and send it over to your house."

"Very well. I am leaving now," the young carpenter said and returned home with the black leather chest.

After he arrived at home, he opened the chest and saw a pile of contracts and title deeds for the land that his cousin owned. It had everything his cousin owned.

"How did you know that this black chest was filled with everything he owns?" he asked his wife with surprise.

"Why can't I know? Is there anything I don't know? With this chest, your whole family can live without worries," she said with a smile.

"I am so grateful that you care about us so much," he said, "but I would rather keep you forever than have any of these things."

He began to cry as he was talking.

"I have no other choice." She also began to choke with tears. "When I came, I had an agreement with my father. I must return home after three years."

They were so sad and hugged together, weeping, in tears.

Before long, two sedans sent by the cousin arrived at the house. The cousin's wife and concubine got out of one of them. They were still very young and beautiful. After the carpenter received them, they became part of his family.

His wife was already dressed and had makeup and now stepped into the other sedan. The husband and wife separated with tears. Then the sedan departed very quickly.

In the meantime, the cousin was glad to have exchanged a wife and a concubine for a fairy from the celestial world. He was so happy in his heart that he held a big banquet for many friends and relatives. They all toasted to him, one after another, and he drank several dozen cups of wine. When the banquet was over, he was so drunk that he fell to the ground like a pile of mud. But he then remembered his new fairy-like wife. He fumbled and climbed up into his room where she was sitting upright on the bed, solemn and beautiful. But when he climbed onto the bed and wanted to touch her, she said to him, with a serious look, "Don't be like this. Since we are now husband and wife, why do you behave like this? I will go and bathe now."

She then walked toward the backyard.

"Do you want to take a shower? I'll ask the maids to prepare hot water," he said, but simply followed her.

They came to the backyard, where there was a small pond. Once she reached the pond, she lifted her gown, jumped into the pond, and immediately turned into a carp. When the cousin saw with his own eyes that his beautiful wife suddenly turned into a carp, he was immediately shocked and awoke from his drunken condition. But this is not strange enough yet. Then the water in the pond began to rise and soon covered the ground. Indeed, it rose ten feet

high and washed away the cousin's house. Meanwhile the carp swam to the crystal palace under the sea and was reunited with her father.

After all his trials and tribulations, the lucky young carpenter was rewarded with a wife, a concubine, and a son simply because he saved a fish and released it into the sea.

PART TWO

Predestined Love

Once there was a poor man who lost his parents when he was young. Whenever he begged a penny of money, he would lose it in gambling. He lost everything, and no relative wanted to be close to him.

Now that he had no money to gamble, he suddenly thought of an idea to help himself. He ran to his maternal uncle's house and said, "Uncle, uncle! Your nephew is getting married. Please chip in, as your late sister would have wanted you to do."

Therefore, his uncle gave him ten strings of money and said, "Let me know when your wedding feast will take place."

He then ran to his paternal uncle's house and said, "Uncle, uncle! Your nephew is getting married. Please chip in, as your late cousin's brother would have wanted you to do."

His uncle gave him ten strings of money and said, "Let me know when your wedding feast will take place."

Now, he had twenty or thirty strings of money. But within a few days, he lost most of the money, while his uncles kept asking him when the wedding would be held. Eventually, he had no choice but to say, "Tomorrow, tomorrow!"

Then he went to a paper crafts store and asked the craftsman to make a paper bride. Since he was afraid of being seen during the day, he went to pick it up at night. Then, he carried the paper bride on his back. As he passed a tomb, he took a rest and peed. Right after that, he continued on his way. Meanwhile, he felt the paper bride getting heavier, but he did not think much of it. He went straight home, and put the paper figure in the dark corner of his room.

The next day, his uncles came to eat at the wedding feast. After they sat down at the table, the poor man shouted at his room, "Now the elders are here. Come out and make tea!"

As he said this, out came a beautiful young woman. When she walked into the kitchen, his maternal uncle said, "My nephew's wife is indeed beautiful!" His paternal cousin uncle also said, "My nephew's wife is indeed beautiful!"

Now, the poor man was so scared that his heart began to beat fast. He thought to himself, "Is this some kind of ghost coming to harm me?"

When all the uncles left, the poor man did not dare to walk toward the woman. But his bride said, "Why are you afraid of me? Let me tell the truth. I am so-and-so's daughter. I just recently died. When you took a rest next to a tomb, it was mine. As part of my fate, I was doomed to have one month's good fortune with you. So, my soul attached itself to the paper bride and transformed me as you see me. One month from now, I shall be the matchmaker who will procure a wife for you."

Upon hearing these words, the poor man became joyful. He hurried and sent a message to the woman's family and informed them that their daughter had come to life again and he had brought her home as his wife. Immediately, the family sent people over who saw that it was true. Indeed, their daughter was alive.

One month later, her family came over to bring back their daughter. When she was brought to her home, her sister-in-law said, "You should sleep with me tonight!"

But her younger sister said, "My elder sister has been away for such a long time. I have been missing her so much. We two sisters should sleep together tonight so we can chat more!"

So, the two sisters slept together. At midnight, when the young sister turned over, she woke up and kicked her feet. Then, she heard something falling and shouted, "Sister! Sister!"

There was no reply. The younger sister lit the lamp and tried to find her sister, but it was all in vain. There was only a paper person on the bed, and there was a hole as big as a bowl in her hip. The younger sister was horrified. She shouted and called her mother, who ran over, and once she saw the scene, she said, "How come you kicked your sister to death! Now she's been turned into a paper person. What can we do if your brother-in-law wants her back?"

For the next couple of days, the whole family tried to figure out what to tell their son-in-law, but they couldn't think of any good plan except that they asked the younger sister to take the role of her elder sister. The poor man pretended not to be happy about the arrangement, but thought in his heart, "Wonderful! Wonderful! Make it a done deal!"

Of course, now we wish that the poor man will stop gambling from this point on—otherwise his wife will starve.

12 ■ The Human-Bear's Death for Love

Once upon a time, there was an explorer who wanted to go abroad. As soon as he got on a ship and sailed away, the wind became too strong and dangerous. Consequently, the ship had to anchor at the dock of a foreign country, and the captain said, "Those passengers who would like to tour this place can get off now. When the wind changes direction and comes from the southeast, you must return immediately. Then we must depart, and I'll wait for no one!"

The passengers were happy to have this unusual opportunity. Consequently, they got off the ship one by one and found ways to enjoy themselves. Many were relatives and friends and began their tours in groups of twos and threes. The explorer was left alone, and after he got off the ship, he explored the valleys and woods by himself. He enjoyed all the views around him and watched the magpies in the east and the wild geese in the west. What a beautiful scene of mountains and waters! The beauty made him forget about everything, even eating.

A couple of days later, he wandered to a mysterious place, and as he was walking, the southeast wind suddenly began to stir. He then remembered the captain's words and felt shocked. It was as if his heart had been torn apart. Turning around, he ran back to the ship. When he arrived at the dock, however, the ship was gone. Not a single person around at all! He searched back and forth and cast his two big eyes all over the sea as if they could distinguish the ship from the sea waves. But he found nothing, even when it turned dark. Consequently, he fell into despair, with no way to describe his feelings. The endless sea stood in front of him, and behind him were endless mountains and rivers. He was entirely alone. Hopeless, he walked aimlessly toward the mountains. As he was walking, he saw a bear coming toward him. However, he was not afraid, because the bear only gazed at him and smiled. But, when they were side by side, the bear grabbed him and walked toward a cave. The bear had the strength of three men. Once they were in the cave, the bear did not eat him, but made a bed with dry grass and let him sleep on it. The bear treated him very kindly. Every morning, it would leave the cave and block the entrance with big rocks. By evening, the bear came back with lots of peaches and other fruits for him. It turned out that the bear was female. Her male partner had died. Now that she had captured the explorer, she served him very carefully. Gradually, they got along so well that she wanted to marry him. Soon they became husband and wife, and she appeared to be very content.

Two years later, she gave birth to two babies, half-human, half-bear, and so, she thought that now he would never want to leave her. After all, they had their own babies, right? Therefore, she stopped blocking the entrance to the cave when she left as she had done before.

After the explorer had been living there for about three years, he knew that the ship was due to return. Consequently, as soon as he could, he escaped from the cave and ran directly to the dock. It was there that he saw the ship sailing toward him from a good distance. When he waved to the ship, the passengers on the ship thought that he was an animal because he had not shaved for years and looked haggard. Therefore, they refused to approach the dock to pick him up. However, he quickly shouted and told them his story from afar, convincing them to dock the ship. Once they did this, he ran right on to the ship.

But what about the female bear? She returned that day to the cave with lots of marvelous fruits that the explorer had never seen or eaten. On her way back to the cave, she chuckled and danced, but when she entered the cave, she couldn't find him anywhere! She then grabbed the two babies in her arms and searched for him with great frenzy. Just as she arrived at the dock, the ship departed. Tears poured down her cheeks as she moved along the shore back and forth, slapping her chest, stamping her feet, touching her heart, and pointing at the sky. She even raised the babies with her hands to show them to him, but he completely ignored her. As a result, she was so overcome by her grief and pain that she tore the two baby bears into pieces and threw them toward the ship. Soon after this incident, she also threw herself into the sea and died.

13 ■ The Snake Spirit

Once upon a time, there was an old man who had three daughters. One day, the old man had to cut wood in the mountains, and his three daughters asked him to pick some flowers for each one of them. The old man agreed to do this and departed. Once he was in the mountains and about to pick the flowers for his daughters, the snake spirit appeared in the form of a handsome young man and asked the old man, "For whom are you picking the flowers?"

"For my mother," the old man lied.

"Your mother is very old. How could she possibly wear such bright flowers? I don't believe you."

"Oh, I forgot. They are actually for my wife," said the old man, though his wife had died many years earlier.

"For your wife? Then you should pick some other kind of flower."

"Well, . . ." the old man realized it was impossible to lie anymore.

"What? Aren't you going to tell me?"

The old man knew that he had encountered the snake spirit and quickly stuttered, "Oh, yes. Now I remember. They are for . . . my daughters."

"How many daughters do you have?"

"Three," the old man regretted admitting this.

"What do they look like?"

"The eldest has big feet. The second has a pockmarked face. Only the third looks pretty good."

"Then I want to marry your third daughter. You must bring her here tomorrow. The deal is done. Otherwise, well, I will eat you up!"

With these words, he left.

The old man did not dare to say anything, and now, he had to return home with a very sad face.

"Father, where are the red flowers?"

The three daughters were waiting at the door for the flowers.

"Here they are. But, . . ."

The daughters were confused, not knowing what had happened. So, the old man had to tell them what had happened to him, without missing a word. Then, the old man asked the eldest daughter, "Would you be willing to marry Snake, or would you rather let him eat me up?"

"I'd rather let Snake eat you up," she said with anger and then left.

"How about you?" he asked the second daughter.

"I'd rather let Snake eat you up," she said, believing that it was a dangerous thing to marry Snake.

Now the saddened old man had to turn to his third daughter.

"I'd rather marry Snake than let you be eaten up!" she said firmly to her desperate father.

The next day, the two elder sisters gladly used their red cord to help the third sister braid her hair. They also decorated her hair with the beautiful red flowers that their father had brought with him the day before. Then the old man brought her to Snake.

"How stupid she is! She wants to marry Snake even though he will devour her. No doubt, she will be eaten up," the eldest and middle sister said to each other.

Then the third sister and Snake became husband and wife. They were happily in love. Snake was wealthy, and all the things in the house were made of gold and silver. When the middle sister saw this, she became envious.

One day, when Snake was not at home, the middle sister dressed herself up and went to see her younger sister. As she stepped across the threshold, she asked, "What's making that ding-dong sound?"

"The gold doorsteps and silver doorsteps make the ding-dong sound."

As the middle sister entered the third sister's bedroom, she asked, "What's making the ding-dong sound?"

"The gold tent hooks and silver tent hooks are making the ding-dong sound."

The middle sister thought that she was in heaven when she saw all the endless things to use and endless food to eat. She then said, "Sister, let's look into the mirror and see who is more beautiful."

In the mirror, the second sister looked so coarse and ugly with pockmarks all over her face that she became extremely angry. She then thought of a plan, and said, "Sister, why don't we exchange our clothes and then look into the well to see who is more beautiful?"

The third sister was naïve and young after all, and therefore, she simply followed the suggestion. When they got to the well, the middle sister suddenly pushed the third sister into the well and then quietly waited for Snake to come home.

When Snake returned home, he noticed that his wife looked different, though her clothes were the same.

"How come your face now has those pockmarks?" he asked.

"I took a nap on the hemp-bag, and it left those marks."

"How come your feet are so big now?"

"I carried some buckets of water today, and they puffed up."

蛇太郎

林蘭編

民間童話第六集

上海兒童書局刊

Snake stopped questioning her, and just at this time, the third sister, who had been pushed into the well and had been transformed into a black bird, arrived and cried out: "Shame on you, sister! Shame on you, sister! Shame on you, sister!"

Snake felt strange and then asked the bird, "If you were my wife at one time, then fly into my sleeve!"

Indeed, it was very weird, for the little black bird indeed flew into his sleeve, and all he could think to do was to put her into the birdcage. But she continued, "Sister, shame! Sister, shame!"

The middle sister was helpless and could not do anything about it.

One day, Snake had to go out to do something, and the bird continued crying out, "Sister, shame! Sister, shame!"

The middle sister could not tolerate her anymore. So, she killed the bird. When Snake returned, the bird became delicious meat in the pot. As they were eating her flesh, Snake kept saying, "Yum, this is delicious!" But when the middle sister ate, there was no meat, only bones. Later, they dumped the bones into the ground outside the house, and on this spot, a loquat (*pipa*) tree sprouted. Every time thereafter, when Snake ate a loquat fruit, it tasted sweet and delicious. Every time when the middle sister ate one, it turned into manure.

14 ■ The Garden Snake

Once there was an old man who had three daughters. None of the daughters had been married yet. One day, the old man went to cut wood in the mountains. A garden snake shed its skin and made a big net out of it to catch anyone who walked by the garden. Well, the old man fell into the trap, and just as the snake was about to devour the old man, he cried and said, "I don't mind being eaten, but my three daughters will certainly starve to death. Alas! How can they be helped?"

"What? You have three daughters?" the snake said, after hearing the old man's words. "If you let me marry one of them, I won't eat you."

The old man had to agree. When he returned home, he told his three daughters what had happened to him. He then asked the eldest daughter what she thought about it, and she replied,

"I would prefer not to marry the garden snake even if it means that the snake will devour you."

The old man then asked his second daughter, and she responded, "I would prefer not to marry the garden snake even if it means that the snake will devour you."

Finally, the old man had to ask his third daughter, and she replied, "I prefer to marry the garden snake rather than let the snake devour our father."

So, the old man had his third daughter dressed for the wedding and brought her to the garden snake. After the wedding, the garden snaked treated his wife extremely well and was extremely gentle to her. Indeed, the young couple got along very well and were deeply in love.

After about half a year, the third daughter began to miss her father and sisters and wanted to visit them. But she was a little concerned that she would not find the way home. Therefore, the garden snake himself escorted her all the way. He also brought a bag of sesame seeds with him and spread the seeds along the way. He told her that, when the sesame seedlings sprouted, she could then easily follow the path and come back home.

Once she arrived at her old home, the third sister was very glad to see her father and sisters again. After she had married the snake, the third sister had enjoyed a life of luxury. She had gold and silver flower pins for her hair and wore silk and embroidered clothes. The eldest sister saw her and became jealous. She even regretted that she had not married the garden snake. So, she asked the third sister to go out and look into the well so that they could see who was more beautiful. Looking into the well, the eldest sister saw that the third sister was ten times more beautiful than she was. But she would not admit it. Therefore, she asked the third sister to go to the riverbank and look into the river. Again, the third sister was more beautiful. The eldest sister said, "What you wear on your hair are beautiful things, and what you wear on your body are also marvelous clothes. Of course, I cannot compare with you. If you let me wear those things, then we can compare again and see who is more beautiful."

The third sister took off her jewels and good clothes and gave them to the eldest sister. After the eldest sister put on those jewels and clothes, she did not go and look into the river. Instead, she pushed the third sister into the river and drowned her. She then went home and pretended to weep, "My sister fell into the river by accident, and she has drowned."

Now, the eldest sister went to the road every day to see if the sesame seeds had blossomed. One day, she indeed saw the green seedlings. She was very happy and then followed the sesame seeds all the way to the garden snake's home. When the snake saw that she was wearing all the same jewels and clothes, he noticed, however, that her face and body were not quite the same. Consequently, he asked: "You have been away for a long time. What have you been doing at home? You seem to have lost your looks."

"Don't mention it. When I returned home, they all forced me to do the hard and dirty work. This is why I look so ragged."

"But how come you have pockmarks on your face?"

"Well, one day when I was working in the field to thresh and dry soybeans, I fell," the eldest sister said, "and my face hit the beans. So, I got those little scars."

"How come your hands are so coarse?" he asked.

"I had to push and pull the grinding mills every day," she said.

"How come your feet are so much bigger?"

"I had to tread in the rice field every day," she replied.

Since the garden snake believed her, she continued to pretend to be his wife.

One early morning, the eldest sister was combing her hair at the window. Suddenly, a little black bird cried out at her, "Using my comb and combing your dog hair! Using my mirror and looking at your dog face!"

Immediately, the eldest sister knew that the bird had been transformed from the third sister's soul. She was very angry and desperately threw the comb at the bird, killing the bird, which fell off the tree. Then she picked it up, and cooked it in a pot. When the garden snake came back home, they both ate it. It turned out that when the garden snake was eating, every bite he had turned into delicious meat, but every bite she took turned into bones. She knew it was the third sister's magic. So, she poured out everything from the pot in the yard. The next day, a jujube tree grew from the place where she had poured the soup. It soon began to yield fruit. She picked many jujube dates, and ate them together with the garden snake. Every jujube date he ate was delicious, but every time she ate a date, it turned into dog poop. She was so angry that she cut down the tree and made a washing-stick out of the tree branch. Every time she hit the clothes when she went washing, the clothes were torn apart. She then stuck the stick into the stove and burned it.

Somehow her nearby relatives sensed that something was awry. Consequently, they went to the house and smelled smoke in the kitchen. When they walked inside, they suddenly saw a shining gold figure rise out of the ashes. So, they secretly wrapped it up with their clothes and brought it back home, where they hid it in a bamboo chest. Every day, when they returned from work, they saw that their cotton had been made into spinning thread. They wondered how that could happen, since the door was locked and nobody could enter. One day, they pretended to go out, but then hid underneath the window so that they could peek inside. Then they saw the gold figure walk out of the chest and turn into an extremely beautiful girl. She then began to spin the cotton into thread. When they recognized that she was the third sister, they were surprised and thrilled. So, they ran into the room and grabbed hold of her. Immediately, they shouted and called the garden snake and the eldest sister.

Although the garden snake recognized that it was the third sister, he felt confused and puzzled since the eldest sister was present as well. The relatives asked the three of them to let their hair down and loosen it. The two persons whose hair intertwined would indicate who the true husband and wife were. The garden snake's hair and the third sister's hair intertwined, but the garden snake's hair and the eldest sister's hair would not intertwine. Once the garden snake knew that the third sister was his original wife and the eldest sister was in disguise, he suddenly swallowed the eldest sister. Then he and the third sister became husband and wife again as they had been and remained so until the end of their days.

Once upon a time, there was a young couple who were happily in love. Before long, the wife died. The husband missed her so much that he set his heart to search for her. He heard people saying that, after a person died, he or she changed into a ghost, and all ghosts lived in a place called Ghost Town. Consequently, he departed for Ghost Town and walked a long way before reaching the vicinity of the town. Once there, he found an inn and sat down to ask the innkeeper how to get to the Ghost Town.

"I had a good wife," he said, "but she died, and I want to find her. How can I find her?"

"You can get there by tomorrow. From here to there, it's one day's walk. If you hurry, you can get back within a day. When you leave here, go straight ahead, and you will come upon a well. She will surely come there to fetch water. At that time, you will see her."

The husband remembered the innkeeper's words and set off the next morning. He got there, and sat there patiently waiting for her. Before long, his wife walked to the well, just as the innkeeper said she would. Oh, indeed! Here she came! Here she came! He saw a beautiful woman walking toward him with a water bucket in her hand. Her body was exactly like that of his wife. She was indeed his wife. He called her by name, and held her by her arm. But she appeared to be a stranger and did not know him. Without even looking at him, she fetched water and left. He felt depressed and had to return to the inn. When he saw the innkeeper, he told him how ungrateful she was and hadn't even looked at him.

"Oh, I see," the innkeeper said. "Don't worry. I forgot to tell you something yesterday. When you go there again tomorrow, bring some coins with you. When she comes to fetch water, throw your coins into the bucket. Then she will talk to you."

After spending the night at the inn, the husband went happily to wait for his wife the next morning. Everything went smoothly. As she walked to the well, he threw the coins into her bucket. She then talked to him. She seemed to have still remembered that they were husband and wife. But she said, "Why don't you go back? It doesn't make sense. I have already become a ghost. We cannot become husband and wife again!"

She then left sadly. However, he wouldn't let her go and followed her closely. The sun was setting, and soon they entered a small village, where she stopped and said, "My dear! You don't need to follow me anymore. The house in the front is my home. I am already married to the ugly Night Demon. He has a cow-head and a horse-face and is extremely ferocious. If you go into the house, he will eat you up. You'd better return before he comes back!"

The husband refused to leave her, and she said with great sorrow, "If this is the case, you can hide in my house. When he asks, I will tell him that you are my brother. If he cooks for you, you should first look at me. If I eat, then you can eat. You must be careful because most of those things are earthworms and toads, and they don't taste good."

They then entered the house. In just the blink of an eye, Night Demon returned. As soon as he entered the house, he yelled, "I smell the taste of a stranger! The taste of a stranger! Who came here?"

He was yelling while searching around wildly. Quickly, the wife said, "My brother has come to visit!"

"Oh, that's why. My brother-in-law has come! Hurry and make the tea and a meal!"

They met and followed the protocol. Night Demon did not eat him up. So, the husband then stayed for about ten days. It turned out that Night Demon had to go to the realm of hell to work every day. They all got along well. However, at one point, the wife said, "My dear! Since we cannot become husband and wife here, why should we stay here like this? Why don't we escape?"

So, they decided to escape. They walked for about ten days and came to a village in the human world. As they came to a house, she said, "I am very thirsty. You stay right here for a moment. I'll go in and have some tea. Here is a coin. Let's break it into halves and each of us keep one half."

Then she walked into the house, and the husband waited outside. He waited and waited until it was completely dark, but she still did not come out. He became anxious and ran into the house, where he asked the house owner whether a woman had entered. The owner of the house said, "No!"

"What? She obviously walked into your house!"

Just at this time, the owner's wife gave birth to a baby girl. They heard the baby crying. The husband then insisted on staying in the house as a house servant. It became strange. Whenever someone carried the baby girl, she would cry loudly without stopping. But when this house servant carried her, she would stop crying. As she grew and then turned seventeen years old, the house servant accidentally opened the girl's hand, which she had not been able to open since her birth. He saw a half coin in her hand. He took out his half coin. The two halves matched perfectly as one coin. Then they got married and became husband and wife.

Once there was a peasant who got up very early every day even before the rooster crowed. He would then carry a hoe to work in the field. He was like this every day, and it became his unchangeable habit. He would sing the local tunes as he walked out of the village, and then shout the local drama songs. True to his habit, he would first sit at the edge of the field and smoke a pipe of tobacco before beginning to work. This is what he did day-in and day-out.

One day, as he was smoking, a woman in mourning dress suddenly appeared in his field. She had morning dew all over her body, and when he saw her walking in his field, he felt very angry and shouted, "Who are you? How come you don't walk on the road but in my field?"

"Please don't get angry," she explained. "You see that I am in mourning dress. Can't you see that I've lost my husband? Now I would like to find a diligent and capable peasant to become my husband. But how can a peasant demonstrate that he is diligent and capable? The only way to find such a man is by walking in the fields. This is why I am searching in your field. Do you understand now?"

He nodded, and thought to himself, "Oh, she is looking for a husband. My wife died not long ago. If I can become her husband, what else could be better? Everyone in the village praises me as a diligent man, and my crop in the field grows better than all others. I must be qualified."

Thanks to this encounter, the woman had the same thought. So, they then got married.

However, it turned out that the woman was not really human, but a goblin. She was sent by the sun to harm this peasant because he got up every day before the sun rose and thus made the sun jealous. But the peasant had no way of knowing this.

After the goblin and the peasant were married, their life was full of joy. The peasant kept her company all the time from morning till evening, talking and laughing. She treated him just as any virtuous wife would treat her husband, and she showed no sign of her original goblin character. However, one day, a fortuneteller came to their village. He was good at telling fortunes from a person's face. When he met the peasant on the street, he kept staring at his face, and the peasant felt confused.

"Why do you always look at me like that?" the peasant asked.

The fortuneteller smiled, and said, "Don't be surprised. I see that your life will end in seven days. There is a strong sign of a goblin on your face. You must have married forty-two days ago, right?"

"That is right. Forty-two days," replied the peasant.

"The woman you married must be a goblin. She came to harm you, and this is why she married you. I don't know whether you believe it . . . seven times seven, you have forty-nine days to live. Then you will die," the fortuneteller stated as if it were the truth.

Now the peasant became very scared and asked, "Is there any way to save me?"

"Yes, indeed," the fortuneteller said and took out two yellow ribbons with spells to avoid all demons and goblins. He gave them to the peasant, and said, "Go home. On your forty-ninth day, early in the morning, you are to paste one ribbon on the door, and the other on the bed. You must also buy some cinnabar powder. Then hold the cinnabar water in your month. If you see something scary, then spit on it. This is how you can avoid the peril."

After saying these words, the fortuneteller disappeared.

On the forty-ninth day, the peasant got up very early and pasted the ribbons just as the fortuneteller told him to do. His wife also got up unusually early. When the peasant opened the window, he saw her sitting in the yard. She removed her head and put it on the stool to comb her hair. After combing her hair, she put her head back on her neck. The peasant was scared to death. He quickly closed the window, ran to the kitchen, and took a knife. Then he drank some of the cinnabar water and held it in his mouth, waiting quietly for something scary to happen.

Finally, the scary thing happened as he watched his wife. After she combed her hair, she walked toward the house. But, when she stepped through the door, she screamed as if she had been stabbed by a knife. She saw the spell pasted on the door and stood there numbed. Meanwhile, white hair immediately grew out of her body. Her mouth changed to a bloody basin while her head was turning into a jujube date pit. She became taller, totally different from what she was like before. Now, the peasant boldly walked out and quickly spit the cinnabar water onto her face, causing her immediately to fall on the ground. Then he stabbed her in the heart, and out gushed some blood. Within seconds, she died, and from then on, the peasant never married again and remained single for the rest of his life.

17 ▪ The Marriage of a Human and a Ghost

Once upon a time, there was a frivolous young man who often seduced young married women. One evening, he was walking alone in the field. Suddenly, a young lady came walking toward him. She was extremely beautiful and had a charming gait. The moment he saw her, his soul soared up into the sky. He did every-

thing possible to please her and asked her to marry him. She finally shyly agreed. It was love at first sight for both of them, and they began to live together without the introduction of a matchmaker.

Time flew by quickly. They even had a baby son who was tender and white. The young woman was also very attentive to her mother-in-law. So, the whole family lived happily together.

One day, however, something unfortunate happened when a fortuneteller came to their village. He passed by their house and was very hungry. So, he begged for some food. The mother-in-law was a kind-hearted woman, and gave him a full meal. He was grateful. Then he saw her grandson was thin and pale, and the baby had a ghost sign. He whispered to the old lady and said, "I am very grateful to you. Unfortunately, I have nothing to pay you back for your kindness. But I have one thing to ask. Where did your daughter-in-law come from?"

As soon as the old woman heard this, she felt strange and surprised.

"When she walks over the threshold," the fortuneteller continued, "does she jump with both feet? Does she leave footprints behind when she walks?"

The old woman began to understand. Then he told her, "Your daughter-in-law is not a human, but a ghost. If you don't get rid of her soon, your son and grandson will be in danger."

The old woman was completely shocked, and began to beg him for help.

"I am grateful for your kindness," he said again, "and I am willing to help you. You must tell your son not to believe her love, nor to be afraid. She will eventually say that she wants to go back to her maternal home. In fact, she has already reserved some pork from a butcher. So, I shall give you three spells. One is for your grandson to carry with him; one is to be pasted on the door after she leaves the house; and the last one is for your son. You must tell your son to make sure that when they get to her maternal home, he must let her enter the house first and then paste the spell on the door. If he does that, everyone will be safe. If you don't believe me, I can give you two other spells. You must ask your son to burn the first of the spells after she falls asleep. She will become dry bones. Then he is to burn the second one, and she will be restored to the human shape. Your son must never show any fear."

The old woman received these spells with great apprehension, and that evening she gave them to her son. When everyone fell asleep, he got up quietly. He burned one spell and bravely stood up and looked at the bed. Indeed, he saw an entire skeleton! It was so creepy that he quickly burned the other spell. Then he saw a beautiful woman in bed with long and loose hair as well as a natural smile. She appeared even more beautiful. But he couldn't help but tremble.

Before long, she indeed wanted to return to her maternal home. They all appeared very happy, preparing gifts. He went to the butcher to buy some pork, but the butcher told him that his wife had already reserved a lot. So, he took the pork back home. He himself carried their young son and walked ahead of her, step by step. Since she was a ghost, they set off at night. After walking for a long time, they arrived at a big mansion. She asked him to enter, but he insisted she enter first. She wanted to carry the baby, but he refused to give her the baby. Then many people came out of the house to welcome them. She then had to walk in first. He quickly took the spell from his pocket and pasted it on the door, and then walked in. He ate and drank a lot, and soon fell asleep.

The next day, his mother looked for his return, but he did not arrive. She asked many villagers to search for him. Soon, they found a grave, and he was lying inside with grasshoppers and tadpoles stuck in his mouth. The baby was next to him. A spell had been pasted on the gravestone. Everyone began shouting and yelling. He then woke up and rubbed his eyes as if he had had a long dream. When his son grew older, his eyeballs were turbid and foggy, showing a non-human sign.

18 ■ The Ghost Marriage

Once there was a young man who worked as a clerk at an inn. Since some people owed him money, he went out one day to collect the payments for the debts. While walking alone in a wild field in a valley, it suddenly turned dark, and all he could glimpse were the mountains to the east and west. He walked and walked, but could not find his way out of the valley. Just as he began to feel panicky, he saw a house in the distance. Light was coming from a window. Therefore, he thought to himself, "It's dark and hard to find my way back to the inn. I'd better ask the family to put me up for the night, and then I can return to the inn tomorrow morning."

He followed the light and came to the house. When he looked inside from one of the windows, he saw a young woman reading in the lamplight. He then knocked at the door. Soon the woman opened the door, and he explained that he would like to stay overnight. She agreed immediately. "But," she said, "there is only one bed here."

"I can sit on the stool for the night," the clerk said.

"It's better that I sit and you go to sleep. You have a long way to walk tomorrow," she responded.

He declined repeatedly, but she insisted. He had no choice but to sleep on the bed.

He laid down with his face toward the inside, but she insisted that he face outward. He refused. However, this time she pulled him, and they struggled with each other. After a while, he managed somehow to fall asleep.

In the morning, some villagers got up early, passed by the place, and saw a young man lying next to a coffin. There was an account book next to his head and a rope for tying a bag hanging halfway out. When they woke him, he opened his eyes and was startled.

"How come I am here? I was sleeping on the lady's bed last night!" he said.

"You must have met a ghost," they said.

He went back to the innkeeper, who scolded him, "Why did you stay overnight outside after collecting the payments? You must have done something wrong."

The clerk had to tell him all the details about what had happened to him. Then, the innkeeper asked where this place was. The clerk told him, and the innkeeper thought a while and said, "I see. That was the coffin of someone's daughter. She was promised to wed you when she was little. However, she died when she was young and was buried there. You were predestined to be husband and wife.

The clerk went back home and told his parents about it. After some discussion in the family, he took her spirit tablet to her grave and held their wedding.

金田雞

編蘭林

Golden Frog had a wife, who often killed their chickens and ate them. She would then say that the chickens had been stolen. After a long while, Golden Frog began to suspect his wife. He made an excuse to go out, but hid behind a window in the back room. He peeked a few times, and, indeed, finally, he saw her kill a chicken and eat it, but he said nothing.

When he later returned home, his wife said to him as usual, "Damn! Another chicken was stolen today."

"Oh? Damn!" Golden Frog pretended to be surprised. Then he went to the stove and picked up the small salt jar and a pair of chopsticks. He walked over to his wife and said, "I am going to use my old trick and do some fortunetelling to figure out who stole the chicken."

His wife was surprised to hear that, since she did not know what tricks he could perform. All she could do was to watch speechlessly, while Golden Frog hit the salt jar with chopsticks and said, "Salt jar! Lo, lo, lo! The chicken feather fell in the ashes in the hearth. Salt jar! Goo, goo, goo! The chicken meat is stored in a cabinet in the corner of the kitchen."

After he did the fortunetelling, he went over to the cabinet in the corner and took out the chicken meat, and then he dug out the feather from the ashes.

"You are so cheap!" he scolded his wife. "Who put those things there?"

She was so humiliated that she ran back to her parents' home. At that time, her elder brother was plowing in the field about one mile from their house. When he saw his sister running home, he put away the plow, tied the cow to a tree next to the field, and accompanied his sister.

Golden Frog realized that his wife had gone back to her parents' home. Therefore, he chased her, and when he arrived at the field, he saw the plow and the cow and was afraid that they would be stolen. Consequently, he put the plow into the water at the east corner of the pond near the field and tied the cow to a tree in the woods.

Now, Golden Frog entered his mother-in-law's house and told his mother-in-law about her daughter's bad deed. As they were quarreling, the brother arrived home and said his plow and cow were missing and asked his brother-in-law to do some fortunetelling. Then Golden Frog took chopsticks to tap a salt jar and said, "Salt jar! Lo, lo, lo! The plow is in the water at the east corner of the pond. Salt jar! Goo, goo, goo! The cow is tied to a tree in the woods."

Indeed, they found both the plow and the cow. Now, his mother-in-law was convinced that her daughter had eaten those chickens, and Golden Frog's wife also admitted this. Before long, the word about Golden Frog's feat of fortunetelling spread all over the place.

Just at that time, the county governor's daughter lost her ring with a gem on it. The governor heard that Golden Frog's fortunetelling was very effective, so they sent two guards to invite him over that night. Since the order came from the county governor, he dared not refuse to go. As he followed the two guards, it became very cloudy and was about to rain. With great worries, Golden Frog looked at the dark sky and could not help but sighing, "Oh, my! What a dark day and black ground! Someone must be doomed to die today."

The two guards happened to be called Dark Day and Black Ground! They heard Golden Frog's exclamation and quickly kneeled down before him, "Oh, Golden Frog! Please pardon us! We are the ones who stole the ring with the gem!"

"Where did you put it?" Golden Frog pretended to be calm. "Speak out quickly, and then I'll let you two measly dogs live."

"It is underneath the step stone," said Dark Day and Black Ground.

After Golden Frog found the lost ring with the gem, his fame of telling fortunes with the salt jar spread even farther. Before long, the emperor's jade seal was stolen, and nobody could find it even after numerous fortunetellers had sought it. Consequently, the emperor issued an edict to the whole country: whoever found the jade seal would become his son-in-law. The county governor received the edict and then recommended Golden Frog to the emperor.

Golden Frog now sat in the lamplight, holding chopsticks, and staring at the salt jar. He thought back and forth, but could not figure out a way to locate the stolen jade seal. Deep in the night, the emperor sent someone to peek through his window and find out what Golden Frog was doing. Golden Frog noticed that there were people peeking through the upper window, and he cursed with anger, "Don't you look down again and again! Someone must die!"

The person at the window fled, but suddenly, some other person jumped down from the roof beam, kneeled down before Golden Frog, and said, "Oh. Golden Frog! Please forgive my measly miserable life. It was me who stole the jade seal. I heard that you were using the salt jar to do fortunetelling, so I hid behind the beam to watch and heard you say, 'Don't you look down again and again. Someone must die!' Then I knew that you had already discovered who the thief was."

Before he finished speaking, Golden Frog threatened him, and said, "Where is the jade seal? Speak out quickly, then I will let you continue your measly miserable life!"

"It is under the water in the east corner of the city moat," said the thief.

Since Golden Frog had discovered who had stolen the jade seal, he was entitled to marry the princess. On the wedding day, the princess still did not believe his mysterious foretelling. Therefore, she decided to test him by putting an imported treasure into a flower vase and sealed the mouth of the vase. She then asked Golden Frog to tell her where the treasure was; otherwise, he would not be allowed to enter her room. The princess thought to herself, "Since this treasure is imported from a foreign country, nobody in this country has seen it. If he can discover this treasure, he is surely a mighty man."

Meanwhile, Golden Frog sat outside the princess's room. He was very worried and felt hopeless. As he sat there, tapping the salt jar with chopsticks and sighing, "Golden Frog, Golden Frog. You did not die in the high mountains, and you did not die in the vast sea. How come you will just die in this vase?"

At these words, the princess quickly opened the door, pulled him inside, and said, "Oh, my dear! You are indeed a great fortuneteller! There is indeed a Golden Frog inside this vase!"

20 ■ The Toad Son

Once there was a man called Wu Juehu. He was fifty-nine years old and often said to others, "Damn it. I have made more than three thousand offerings with incense in my life, but I've now ended up being called Juehu—descendant-less."

As a result, he was always angry and sometimes scolded his wife. "She is ten years younger than I am," he thought, "but already has gray hair. In a few years, she will be old and may have some illness. Then what to do? If we buy a very small child, it would be too hard to raise it. If we get an older child, it would not be easy to nurture a close relationship. If we adopt one, we won't have a genuine family."

Now, the time had come for the Qing Ming Festival to sweep the tombs. Wu Juehu had a big quarrel with his wife about money. Afterward, he even used what she often said to him to shame her, "Don't blame me. Dare you compare yourself with those who have big families with lots of children?"

At these words, his wife forgot that she had been blamed and began to blame herself for not being able to bear children. She came to her parents' grave and cried her heart out. Just as she was going to return home, she knelt down and murmured. Then, all of a sudden, a toad leaped in front of her.

"Oh, heavens! Bless me with a . . . alas, even a toad-like child that will bring joy to my heart!"

After she uttered these words, she felt a little better, and from then on, she would kneel down at the kang-bed and say those words every night before going to sleep.

Before long, believe it or not, she gave birth to a child whose body was like a toad, but just much bigger. Wu Juehu felt it was too ugly and shoveled it to the ash-pile. But his wife didn't want to give it up. Therefore, she picked it up and washed it clean. Then she carried it in her arms and even breastfed it. After some time had passed, they named it Toad.

Toad's father had a job in a craft store in town, while Toad and his mother stayed at home. Toad grew bigger day by day. Although he didn't speak, he didn't cause any trouble, often playing alone in the yard, jumping and climbing around. His mother was quite content.

Soon Toad was old enough for his mother to arrange a marriage for him, and one day, his mother asked him, "Toad, can you go to town and bring a message to your father?"

Toad nodded.

Their home was about a hundred miles from the town, and Toad's father normally had to walk at least two days to get there. Toad's mother asked the teacher of a family school to write a letter for her, and she prepared enough food for three days. She packed everything and put a package on Toad's back. Of course, Toad could carry those things because he was as big as a sheep crawling on the ground. But Toad moved slowly, because it was stressful to leap and leap. When his mother sent him off to the outskirts of the village, it was already noon. His mother thought, "It took him half a day to get out of the village. How long would it take him to get to the town?" She then whispered to Toad, "Toad, why don't we return home? I'm afraid you won't be able to get to the town."

Toad shook his head, and waved his front leg to his mother to go back. So, she went home alone. In the evening, Toad's father was doing his bookkeeping work in his office in town. Suddenly, he felt something heavy falling on his feet, and he thought, "My eyelids were fluttering the entire day. Does that mean Toad is here now?"

He held the lamp over his feet, and indeed, it was Toad, who was now much bigger. His father took the bag from Toad, opened the letter, and read it carefully. Then he said, "Very good! You'll be married. Now, return home tomorrow morning. I have to finish the work here, and it may take three to five days. After that, I'll be back home."

Toad nodded.

The next morning, Toad's father made breakfast for him, wrote a letter back, and sent him off. By the time the people in his home village finished breakfast, Toad was already home.

His mother saw that he had returned and thought he must be very tired. Therefore, she took down his bag and asked, "Did you get to see your father?"

Toad nodded.

"Then, did you go . . . oh, how fast!"

Toad nodded.

At first, his mother did not believe he had seen his father, but she then saw the envelope and changed her mind. She felt so suspicious that she took it to the teacher and learned that it was written by Toad's father. So, she was happy and thrilled to know that Toad would be married.

Five days later, Toad's father returned home. The bride's family lived about fifty miles away and was poor. They did not know what Toad looked like. Rumors spread to the bride's mother that her son-in-law was rather ugly. But she said, "So long as the person is good, and there is enough food to eat and clothes to wear, it doesn't matter whether he is ugly or handsome."

The time came. Toad and his bride began to stroll down the aisle. The people watching this event all laughed at the groom. The bride seemed quite calm and did not show any disappointment.

After the wedding ceremony, all of the guests and relatives sat at the banquet tables. Toad did not care at all about his appearance. He leaped to the central seat and began taking food to eat. Those guests and relatives all laughed at him. Some people thought, "Such a beautiful girl marrying such an ugly creature. What a bitter fate she has!"

That evening, nobody came to tease the newlyweds as is usually done at weddings. The bride made the bed and was about to sleep. She turned around, and suddenly saw a handsome young man full of smiles! She was so shocked and asked, "Who are you? How come you are here?"

"You don't recognize me?" said the young man. "You were with me just now, and I was very close to you!"

The bride looked around and could not see Toad and realized that the young man had changed from a toad to man. So she asked, "How come you looked like that and now . . . ?"

"That does not matter. When I am in that pearl robe, I will look like that. Taking that off, I am like this."

The bride was extremely content. So, they together spent a very happy night.

The next morning, the young man put on his pearl robe and looked again like a big toad. It turned out that the pearl robe was the skin of a toad. They went on like that for five or six days. During the day, there was a dumb toad, but at night, there was a loving and handsome young man.

On the seventh night, after Toad took off his pearl robe, his wife took it and wanted to take a closer look at how delicately it was made. She pretended to be very curious and got very close to the lamp to turn the pearl robe back and forth. Suddenly she cried out, "Oh, my! It's terrible!"

"What happened?" asked the young man, moving toward her. It turned out that the pearl robe was burned and now had a big hole. He said gently with sorrow, "What a pity! It can't be worn in the future."

From then on, no matter whether it was day or night, Toad was always a handsome young man.

Once there was a family that was not very well-to-do. The husband and wife were both more than thirty years old. However, they had no children, and since they very much wanted to have a child, they went to the temple of the Earth God to pray for a son.

Once there, they knelt down and prayed. "Earth God!" they cried. "For a long time, we have been hoping for a son, but we've yet to have one. You are the most compassionate! Bless us with a son! If not a son, a chicken egg is also just as good."

Soon after, the wife indeed became pregnant. Ten months later, the woman delivered a chicken egg, not a baby. The egg could roll back and forth itself, and when it got cold, the egg would call his mother to hold him on her breast underneath her clothes. The husband felt a little strange and weird, but it was at least better than having nothing.

One day, a young woman from a rich family passed by Egg's house. Consequently, Egg's father quickly put him into his pocket and stood at the gate watching.

When the girl was near the gate, Egg shouted, "Dad! Dad!"

"Egg, what do you want?" the father asked.

"I want the beautiful girl to be my wife," Egg said loudly.

"Egg!" Father said, "If you want to stay alive, don't shout like this."

Egg was upset by his father's scolding and began to weep. After the girl walked away, the father went inside the house, where Egg was crying loudly and incessantly. He cried day and night. The couple felt annoyed and said to Egg with a deep sigh, "Egg! Egg! You cry so much, but it won't help. You should also think about who you are, and who that young woman is. You should think about whether she would be willing to be your wife."

Egg then stopped crying and said, "Dad, all you need to do is to find a matchmaker. Her family will definitely agree."

The couple had no way to deal with Egg. Therefore, they hired two matchmakers to arrange a marriage with the girl's family. In fact, the two matchmakers went and talked with the rich man. The rich man laughed very hard after hearing the matchmakers. Then he pretended to be serious. "If they can build a house with golden pillars and jade beams for my daughter, if they can afford a sedan made of gold and jewels to fetch my daughter, then I will allow my daughter to marry Egg."

The matchmakers returned to Egg's father and told him what they heard from the rich man. Egg was in his father's pocket and heard the matchmakers' words. He instantly shouted out, "Wonderful! Wonderful! I accept all the demands. Go and tell the rich man to allow me to marry his daughter!"

Egg's father was rather worried and reminded him, "We don't even have one copper coin at home. How can we buy those treasures? Your promise really drives me mad!"

"Dad, don't worry. I have ways to get those treasures," Egg said.

The matchmakers returned to the rich man and told him what Egg had said. The rich man had not realized that his demands would be accepted. It was all a joke for him. Now, he had no choice except to allow the gold and jeweled sedan to come and fetch his daughter.

Back at Egg's home, his father asked: "Now that the girl's family has agreed, how can you get such a sedan?"

"Dad, please take a hoe, and bring me to our backyard," Egg said.

The father did what Egg said, and once they were in the backyard, Egg said: "Please go to the east corner where there's a grave with withered grass, and dig it up."

"What? No, no, no!" his father screamed. "This is an ancient grave, several hundred years old. Many old ghosts dwell here. This is where we come every Tomb Sweeping Day on the fifth day of the fourth month and Winter Solstice Day to make offerings and send money to the dead by burning the joss paper."

"Dad," Egg said, "You are fooled by the ancients. That is not a grave of a dead person. It was a site where a rich man buried his treasure when there was a riot. He purposely made it look like a grave to fool others and to leave a mark for himself. But he was killed not long afterward. So, this is why people call it an ancient grave."

At these words, the father began to dig the grave. Indeed, he soon found all the glittering treasures. Before long, a mansion of gold pillars and jade beams was built, and Egg's father bought a sedan of gold and jewels. Now, they waited only for the auspicious day to fetch the beautiful bride.

When the rich man heard this, he was stunned and speechless. Moreover, his daughter cried desperately when she was told she was to become Egg's wife. Soon the shining sedan made of gold and jewels appeared at the gate of the girl's house, and the beautiful girl had to leave her home.

Colorful lanterns were hung in Egg's house, and everything was ready for the bride's arrival. As soon as she appeared, the best men carrying Egg and the bridesmaid bowed to the heavens and earth and then to the parents. This is how Egg and the beautiful girl became husband and wife.

Inside the newlyweds' chamber, the candles were bright and the decorations were charming. The bride sat at the edge of the bed, and Egg was on the bed. Those guests coming for the feast saw this scene and felt pity for the bride and even shed tears.

By midnight, all the guests left. Their parents also returned to their room. Only the bride and Egg were in the chamber. Slowly, Egg began to roll back and forth on the embroidered quilt. Suddenly, there was a bright red light. The eggshell opened, and out popped a handsome young man! Once the bride saw him, she was delighted! Afterward, the young man blew out the candles, and no one learned what happened between Egg and his bride.

The following morning, Egg's mother asked the bride, "Did Egg treat you nicely last night?"

The bride told her the truth.

The mother said, "Why not totally break the eggshell so that this immortal can be in the human world forever?"

The bride thought it was a good idea, and said, "Mother-in-law, I'll break the eggshell without letting him know it."

During the next night, the handsome young man opened the shell and came out. The bride put her hand on the shell and pressed it so hard that the eggshell broke into pieces.

When the young man realized what had happened, he cried, "Alas! Our marriage has come to its end!"

Upon saying this, he disappeared, while the bride cried so hard that she passed out.

22 ■ No Giving Up before Seeing the Yellow River

"No giving up before seeing the Yellow River." You may have often heard this proverb from the elders. But now listen to me: when people use this saying to mean that they have a strong intention to achieve something, it is wrong because they don't know the origin of this saying.

It is a long story, but a meaningful one. Here is the beginning, you need to listen quietly.

There was once an inn, I believe, in a big and crowded city. The owners hired a young man who looked very ugly. The fellows there called him Wu Dalang behind his back, a name for a short and ugly man. In fact, this young man's name was Yang, and he was the sixth sibling in his family. Before long, folks began to call him Yang Liulang, the sixth son of the Yang family. He was not a local person and had moved here from far away.

Liulang was indeed ugly, but he could sing and play musical instruments. The fellows in the inn all said that they had never met such a person who sang so beautifully. He brought a *pipa*-lute and a flute with him to the inn. Every evening after work when the moon was bright and the night was quiet, his fellow workers would ask him to sing and play. They fully enjoyed listening to him. Sometimes, when he played the flute, tears would roll down from their eyes. Then they believed that Liulang was not an ordinary person, but perhaps a kind of spirit or goblin or something like that. He was very humble and honest, and only his appearance was ugly. After a long time, people took him for granted and did not respect him any longer. They just liked his singing.

The inn owner's daughter lived with her mother and younger sister in the backyard of the inn. She was as beautiful as a fairy and was not engaged even though she was already nineteen years old. Whenever she heard the singing from the front yard, she would be filled with joy and begin to dance, full of awe. She thought to herself, "A person who can sing so beautifully must be extremely handsome. What if he has never been engaged! Oh! If I could only have a chance to see him."

She kept thinking about the flute player day and night and began to eat less and less. Finally, she got sick. Her father asked her what sickness she had, but she would assert she wasn't sick. Her mother asked her how she became sick like that, and she would just say she didn't know. But her sickness got worse and worse.

Four or five doctors were consulted, but whenever she was given medicine, she wouldn't take it. If she were forced to take the medicine, she would cry loudly. Her father and mother became extremely worried, but they had no clue about her condition. Soon, she became so weak that she was dying. Her mother held her and asked her what she wanted. Now she told her mother the truth, that she wanted to see the singer just once. Consequently, her mother promised her, and told her father.

Her father talked to Liulang and asked him to see his daughter to save her life. Liulang was both surprised and shy, but in his heart, he was willing to see her. Therefore, he quickly went to the daughter's chamber without dressing up.

The daughter had been sick for a long time and had become much thinner, but she was still very delicate and surprisingly charming. Her mother said, "Look! This is Liulang who has come to see you!"

The daughter raised her head and saw a man standing in front of her bed, both dark and ugly, so she hid herself underneath the quilt and pretended to sleep. Liulang had to withdraw from the room.

When the daughter saw that the man was so ugly, she felt relieved. She was no longer obsessed with him. She gradually got better and better and eventually made a full recovery. But from then on, Liulang fell sick, and got worse and worse. Three months passed, and he seemed to be dying. At first, he said he just had an old problem caused by a stomachache, but now he told the truth to the inn owner and begged him, "I only wish to see her one more time. Then, if I die, I shall have no regrets."

The inn owner told his daughter and urged her to go and see Liulang at least one more time. The daughter thought, "Although he is ugly, when he knew I had become sick because of him, he came over to save my life. I owe him my life. Furthermore, he became sick because of me. Alas, he is dying. Why not show my sympathy to see him one more time."

She then decided to see him the next day.

After lunch on the following day, she dressed extremely well and went to Liulang's small room. It happened that Liulang was asleep. Since she did not want to wake him, she left one of her embroidered shoes next to him and left.

Liulang woke up and saw a delicate shoe next to him. He knew that the daughter had just visited him and sighed, "Oh, how sad! How sad that she came while I was asleep! I don't even have the fortune to see her face one more time. This is my fate. Oh, well . . ."

He felt so depressed and worried that he died without finishing his words. He had no relatives and friends, so the fellows in the inn buried him in a piece of the field outside the city.

About two months later, at sunset, a yin-yang master passed by the inn and wanted to stay overnight. After dinner, people were chatting, and the master suddenly said, "Well, I saw a living treasure, but no one could recognize it!"

"What is it?" the inn owner asked.

"Well, a living treasure is hard to describe. Isn't there a cemetery in the field west of the city gate? In the northeast corner of the cemetery, there is a new tomb less than a hundred days old. Although the person in the tomb is dead, his heart is not dead. If someone digs out his heart, puts it in a jar, and fills it with wine, it will sing loudly. Even the best performer will never be able to sing better than that. Indeed, that is a rare living treasure. However, nobody knows who the owner of the tomb is."

The inn owner heard that and felt both strange and happy. So, he said, "Indeed, the person buried in that tomb was a worker in this inn. He was very good at singing before he died. He was homeless. So, let's open the tomb. No one will mind."

The next morning, the innkeeper told his workers to dig up the tomb. By the time the sun was bright, they came back with that living treasure. The inn owner followed the instructions of the yin-yang master. He put the heart in a porcelain jar and filled it with wine. All at once, there was loud singing from the jar, just like the singing of Liulang before his death. After a while, the inn owner poured out the wine, and the singing immediately stopped. The inn owner was thrilled and told the workers to keep the secret and not to tell it to other people. Only when he felt stressed every day, he would let the heart sing to cheer him up.

The daughter heard that beautiful singing for four or five days and wondered, "That man has been dead for more than two months. Why do I still hear his singing? Perhaps the man who came to see me when I was sick was not the real singer, but my parents purposely asked an ugly man over to make me stop thinking of the singer. It must be so. This singing must be from the real singer. The dead man might be just an ugly fellow in the inn."

This was what she thought, and she became too shy even to ask who the singer was. Sometimes, she sneaked to the front yard to listen to the singer, but she dared not walk in because the room was full of men. One day, the daughter's father invited some friends over to have a good time. There was singing from the front yard again.

The daughter went over to the front yard several times to listen, and wanted to find out who the singer was. As the guests were leaving, she hid behind a window to listen. When the last guest left, her father and brothers also walked out to see the guests off before they got a chance to pour the wine out of the jar. They all left the room. The daughter saw those people had left, but there was still singing in the room. Therefore, she gently pulled the curtain to the door and looked inside. Nobody was inside, but she heard singing from the table. "So strange!" she thought, and then walked to the table and took a look inside the jar. Suddenly, the singing stopped.

From then on, no matter what they did about it, the heart would never sing. The inn owner said that the heart was indeed dead.

Yellow River, in fact, was the name of that girl.

23 ■ The Reward of the Snake

Once upon a time, there was a boy whose family led a well-to-do life. Unfortunately, his father died when he was very young. His mother was very capable and managed to keep the family stable with the money left by his father. She sent her son to a nearby school, and he was diligent. He left home for school early and returned home late. He never caused or encountered any trouble. Therefore, the relations between mother and son were strong and loving. Their everyday life was quite peaceful, but their days were also quite boring and dull.

The boy was very kind-hearted and had great sympathy for all natural life. He was a hard-working student, and the teacher praised him almost every day for his good grades and kind love. Indeed, he would even try to save little animals if they were treated violently or in danger. He also made a hobby of raising them. For example, if a bird got injured, he would capture it and put it in a cage. Then he would try to feed and cure it and would set it free when it had recovered from its injury.

One evening after school, he carried his backpack and walked home. On his way, he suddenly saw a small snake. It was about three inches long with blood all over its body, as if dead. That prompted his curiosity and sympathy. He quickly walked up to it and found that it was not dead, but was still breathing. He knew the little snake must have been attacked by some brutal animal and felt great pity for it. So, he picked up the snake and took a closer look at it. Immediately, he thought of something to help the snake. Therefore, he took out an ink box from his backpack and put the snake into it. Then he went home.

When he arrived home, his mother was waiting for him. She was leaning against the door and asked him why he was later coming home than usual. He told her the truth. His mother did not think that this was anything special. After they were inside the house, he took out some medicine and put in on the snake's wounds. He was very careful and attentive to the snake, hoping it would recover soon.

From then on, he would take the snake with him to school every day. Indeed, he never separated from it. A month later, the snake had fully recovered from its wounds and could recognize him without any difficulty. One day, the boy released the snake in the woods, but it came back to him!

Time flew by quickly. A few years later, the snake grew even bigger, but never separated from the boy. At first, the snake stayed in an ink box, but then was moved to a big jar, and finally to a drawer in his room. When the boy was about to go to school, he would first bring some food to the drawer. Each time he opened the drawer, the snake would stick its head out, and the boy would put food into its mouth. Then the snake would lower its head. This is what they did every day, and the snake never caused any trouble. But when it was hungry or the boy forgot to bring food, it would stretch its head out, as if urging or begging for food.

One year, there was a big imperial examination in the capital city. By then, the boy was already twenty years old. Although he was a student in name, he was quite knowledgeable. When he heard about the examination, he talked to his mother and wanted to participate in the exam. His mother agreed to let him go and take the exam, and so, he chose a date to travel to the capital city.

Now the snake was quite big, but he still raised it. He planned to take the snake in a basket to travel with him. After he packed all his clothes and took enough money for the journey, the date arrived, and he bid farewell to his mother and departed.

In those days, there was no easy way to get to the capital city from his home. There was no vehicle nor boat. Instead, he had to walk. Moreover, he had to climb mountains and cross rivers, and spend months on the road. He was alone all the time, and thus he felt a little lonely. To make matters worse, he had grown up in a tiny village and had never left it before. Now that he was on a long journey, he naturally felt worried and anxious. When he saw the snake, he sighed: "Oh, well. Snake, snake. I raised you ever since you were small, less than three inches long. Now several years have passed, and you are so big. Now, I have to take the exam in the capital city and may not have a chance to return home. In addition, here are the mountains and forests, and I have to walk alone for days to cross them. If I meet a wild beast, I shall certainly die. I feel that I am now at the edge of life, and death can come at any moment. In case I die, you would be stuck in the basket and starve to death. Therefore, I shall let you go now, and you can try to survive by yourself. If I am blessed by the heavens, then I shall come back here to this spot and take you home. So, you can go now."

After saying these words, the young man put the snake on the ground. The snake heard him as if it understood everything. Then, it nodded and went into the forest. As soon as the young man released the snake, he walked alone for more than ten days and finally left the forest and reached a small town. He knew that there were still a lot of days before the exam date, and he was not too far from the capital city. Since it was getting dark, he decided to stay overnight in an inn. Unfortunately, every inn was fully booked. This seemed strange to him, and so he asked the innkeeper, "Why are all the inns full now?"

"You may not know. There is an examination in the capital city this year, and there are many people coming from far away to take the exam. Many people are resting here, and that's why all rooms are taken."

"That's why. But could you find a way to help me?" he asked.

"Oh, sir. I can see you are a traveler, and I cannot blame you. All the cheap rooms are taken. I can't help you. But did you try other inns?" the innkeeper asked.

"I went to all the other inns, and they all said no vacancy. That's why I'd really appreciate it if you could find a way to help me."

"That is very difficult. There is only one small room left because a ghost inhabits it, and we don't let our guests stay there. Other than that, we really don't have any room available."

"Well, that is good enough for me. I don't mind whether there is a ghost or not," the young man said, because he thought he would otherwise have to spend the night outside in the open.

"Sir, I'll give you the room, but you can't blame me if anything happens," said the innkeeper.

"Don't worry. I certainly won't make you responsible," he said.

Therefore, the innkeeper brought him into the room along with his luggage and made the bed for him. Then night arrived, and the young man began to hesitate. It was quiet and deep into the night. He kept thinking about the ghost in the room and began to feel really scared. What if the ghost appeared and he lost his life for nothing? Now, he remembered his old mother at home waiting for him. If he never returned home, how desperate his mother would become expecting him. "Maybe I shouldn't have ever traveled to the exam. I really regret it now," he said to himself.

The wind outside was blowing hard, and it was extremely dark. He sat in the lamplight, and could not help but think of those things. He was extremely sad and worried. But soon he became tired and went to bed, thinking that everything would depend on his fate and luck, and it was simply useless to worry about it. However, he still could not help but long for his old mother. So, he decided not to think of anything at all, and just closed his eyes and fell asleep.

At midnight, he woke up but saw nothing unusual except the wind knocking against the windows outside. Inside the room, the lamplight was as small as a bean, almost swallowed by the darkness. He thought perhaps that would be the situation for the rest of the night.

After midnight, the wind became stronger, and the windows were even shaking and making loud noises. Then the window and door opened by themselves. He woke up in the middle of a dream and was shocked. He sat up and saw a dark thing flying from west to east outside the window, and it was followed by another thing.

They came to his window and stopped. The two things stood at his door, and they looked very scary. He sat on the bed trembling. After a while, the noise began to fade away. The two things seemed to be interwoven and fell on the ground.

Soon the day broke. He had no intention to sleep any more, but quickly got out of bed. When he stood up, he was shocked. It turned out that the two things were one centipede and one snake. Both were dead, but tightly intertwined. He took a close look at them and realized that the snake was the one he raised and just released days ago. It just seemed much bigger. He then felt very grateful to the snake. He saw the snake was stiff on the ground, and the young man felt heartbroken. His tears dropped with sympathy. He then asked the innkeeper to properly bury the snake. Then he set off his journey.

Finally, he reached the capital city and passed the exam! He then became an official in his home county. On his way home, he stopped by the inn and took the snake's body back to his hometown, where he built a tomb for the snake and made an offering. His mother was extremely happy seeing her son back home. She then arranged to have him married and live happily ever after.

24 ■ Everyone Is Content

Once there was a young man who was quietly reading a book to kill time. He was in a gloomy mood because no one wanted to marry him. One day, he read these two lines in a book:

> Everyone is content.
> Human sea is content.

He was confused, "How come I never feel content?"

He pondered his situation for some time but could not understand these two lines. Finally, he decided to go to the West to ask the Old Sage Buddha.

When he passed a large pear orchard, an old man who served as gardener called out, "Where is this handsome young man going?"

"I am going to the West to ask the Old Sage Buddha for the meaning of 'Everyone is content. Human sea is content.'"

"Well, could you do me a favor by asking the Old Sage Buddha a question for me—Why do the pear trees in my orchard only bloom but not yield fruits?"

The young man promised to ask the question.

He walked for a while and saw an old woman accompanying a girl of seventeen or eighteen years old. After learning about the young man's mission, the old woman said, "Could you do me a favor? My daughter is very talented and can do everything well, but she is unable to speak. Could you ask the Old Sage Buddha why she is like that?"

The young man promised to ask this question.

He continued his journey and came to a vast sea, which was impossible to cross. Then a big, red-eyed turtle emerged. The old turtle could speak, and after learning what the young man's mission was, the turtle said, "Could you do me a favor by asking the Old Sage Buddha a question for me? If so, I can carry you on my back across the sea."

"What is your question?"

"Ask why I am still not reborn even though I have already reached the expected time."

"Yes, I will ask this question for you," said the young man.

The old, red-eyed turtle asked him to close his eyes and stand on the turtle's back. Then the young man felt the wind blowing, and they crossed the sea.

The young man arrived at the temple of the Old Sage Buddha, who happened to be answering questions just at that moment. Therefore, the young man walked up to the Buddha and began to ask questions.

The Old Sage Buddha asked, "What are your questions?"

The young man replied, "I passed by a pear orchard, and the gardener asked me to ask you why there are only blossoms but no pears?"

"There is a silver chest on the southeast corner of the orchard. Dig it out, and then the trees will yield pears."

Then the young man said, "I also met an old woman with her daughter, who is very talented, but she is unable to speak. The old woman wanted me to ask you to show her a way to help her daughter."

"She will be able to speak when she meets her husband."

"I then met an old, red-eyed turtle. He asked me to ask you when he can be reborn."

"When the sun rises, if he nods three times to the East, he will be reborn."

The young man asked all the questions for others, but before he asked his own question, the Old Sage Buddha stopped answering questions and withdrew from company. Unfortunately, the young man had come a long way, but didn't get a chance to ask his own question. However, he had no choice but to return home. On the way back, he first met the old turtle and told him what the Old Sage Buddha had said. Then the turtle carried him across the sea and did what the Old Sage Buddha had said and was soon reborn.

Afterward, the young man met the old woman and the girl. He told them what the Old Sage Buddha said. Suddenly, the girl pointed at a flying bird in the distance and said, "Mother, what is that?"

The old woman heard her daughter speaking and was extremely happy. She thought to herself: this young man must be her predestined husband. She then asked the young man, "Are you married?"

"No one has shown an interest in me," he replied sadly. "A single man is like a lonely island."

"I think you and my daughter are predestined. If you don't mind that she is not all that beautiful, I'd like you to marry her. Are you willing?"

The young man agreed, and later he met the gardener of the pear orchard. After he told him what the Old Sage Buddha had said, the gardener replied, "All right. Let's go together. If we dig up the silver chest, we two divide what's inside."

Indeed, they dug up the silver chest, and the pear trees began to yield pears. The young man now had a wife and lived happily ever after. He then understood the meaning of "Everyone is content. Human sea is content."

PART THREE

The Hatred and Love of Siblings

民間童話之一

怪兄弟

林蘭 編

When old Wang died, his two sons, Bao (Treasure) and Fa (Wealthy), had to divide their father's inheritance, which was nothing but a simple cow used for plowing. Bao said to his younger brother, "We don't have to divide the cow. I have an idea. If you can run to the cow, jump on its back, and sit there, then the cow belongs to you. If you can't do that, it will belong to me."

Fa was still young and not very bright. He was honest, however, unlike his elder brother. Fa never quarreled with others, but his brother would take the slightest chance to cheat all the time and would even cheat his younger brother. Therefore, when Bao made this proposal about the cow, Fa knew that his brother would try to cheat him. However, since Fa was afraid of his elder brother's temper, he agreed and nodded. The next day, the deal was made. Bao asked Fa to try first. Fa did. But it was impossible to jump and sit on the cow's back with his small body. Then it was Bao's turn. He jumped and easily sat on the cow's back. The result was clear: the cow belonged to Bao, and Fa got only a big flea for his endeavor.

Now, the two brothers separated. Bao built a house and began to plow the field with the cow. Since Fa did not have his brother's skills, he had to wander about the village every day looking for work. Meanwhile, he tied a rope on his only property, the flea, which was by now as big as a sparrow. He walked around with the flea on a leash and enjoyed doing this very much. Bao saw him like that, but he ignored him and never helped him.

One day, Fa took a walk and rested at the gate of a house, holding the leash on the flea, which was creeping back and forth. Suddenly, a large rooster came out of the house and saw the big flea. Of course, the rooster thought it was his food and pecked it to death. Once the rooster swallowed the flea, Fa knew that it was in the rooster's stomach. Consequently, he began weeping loudly, causing the owner of the house to come out and ask, "What's the matter?"

Fa stood up and, with tears in his eyes, cried out, "Terrible! Your rooster swallowed my flea! Give me back my flea!"

"I'm so sorry," the owner of the house replied with sympathy. "Since we don't have a flea, we can only give you the rooster to pay you back!"

Fa accepted the apology and the rooster. Then, he tied the leash to the rooster's leg and walked away.

A few days later, when Fa took the rooster to stroll along the streets, he arrived at a quiet corner and stood at the gate of a rich family's house. Suddenly, a dog ran out and barked at him. Fa didn't pay much attention to the dog. But the dog then bit the rooster to death! Fa became so upset that he began to moan and cry loudly. Indeed, his weeping was so sad and loud that a kind-looking old man came out of the house and asked, "What's wrong, young man? What has caused you to weep like this?"

"Your big yellow dog has bitten my rooster to death!" Fa cried without stopping.

"Oh, is that it? I'll tell you what I'll do. I'll give you the dog to compensate for your loss."

Fa had no choice, but took the dog and walked away.

Interestingly, after following Fa, the dog became so capable that he could plow the field and tread the watermill, and was even stronger than a cow. The dog was also very obedient and considered Fa his only master. From then on, Fa stopped wandering around. He began to work for other families and plow their fields. As he said to one landowner, "My dog has the same skill as a cow. With this dog, you don't need a cow."

"That's a joke! In my entire life, I've never heard that a dog can plow a field. Don't tell lies to me!"

"It's true," Fa said. Then he made a bet with the landowner. If the dog could plow the field, then the landowner would give the field to Fa; if the dog could not plow the field, then the dog would belong to the landowner, and, furthermore, Fa would not get any wages. But the result was clear: Fa won. Fa got a few acres of land, while the landowner could only accept his bad luck.

Fa worked in his field, but many people felt it strange that he used his dog to plow. However, since the dog showed he could do the work, they asked whether the dog could tread the watermill. Fa said yes, but those people did not believe him. Therefore, they made bets with different things. Some bet wood, some bet tiles and bricks. But Fa was bold and said, "If I lose, you all can take my land and divide it among yourselves."

Once they all agreed on the deal, Fa told the dog to stop working in the field, but to tread the watermill. The dog seemed to understand his words, and indeed, began to tread the watermill. Everybody was stunned. They all exclaimed, "Incredible! You've won all the bets!" So, now Fa could build a house near a field, where the dog could do his plowing. The news spread all over the village, and Fa's elder brother Bao also learned about it. By then, Bao had already married a wife from a rich family. They lived a well-to-do life. When he heard about his brother's success, he became jealous. He went to Fa's house and said, "Brother! Your dog can plow the field. I like it very much. My cow is now sick. Can you lend me your dog for a few days? There is a lot of work to do in the field!"

"Of course, of course," Fa said with respect, for he still cared for his brother. Therefore, Bao took the dog and left without saying a word of thanks.

After Bao took the dog home, he did not give the dog anything to eat, but began to let the dog work in the field. The dog barked at him and did not move. Bao lost his temper and yelled at the dog, "You cheap dog. My house is much better than Fa's, why don't you work for me? You are really a despicable low animal."

Still yelling, he took a stick and began beating the dog. How could the poor dog tolerate such a beating? Fa had never hit him, even once. So, in less than three days, the dog died from Bao's beating. Bao saw the dog dead, but didn't feel bad at all. He even felt happy. He dug a hole in the wild field and buried the dog under a tree.

When the bad news arrived and Fa learned that his beloved dog was dead, he almost fainted. He dashed to the grave and cried loudly, holding and shaking the tree. The tree's dry leaves began to fall, turning into gold, silver, and jewelry as they landed on him. Fa was grateful and excited. Since it was getting dark, he took all the gold, silver, and jewelry back home.

Once this news reached his elder brother Bao's ear, he was so jealous that he went to the dog's grave and pretended to cry while he embraced and shook the tree. He hoped to get a lot of gold, silver, and jewelry as Fa did. He shook the tree very hard. Indeed, many things fell off the tree, but they were not gold, silver, and jewelry. They were small, fierce, and poisonous snakes and centipedes. They surrounded Bao and began to bite him. Bao was so scared that he sprinted back home.

When he arrived, he was already sick. As his illness became more and more serious, he went to many doctors and fortunetellers, and used up all of his money and properties. Finally, he died. His wife, an unfaithful woman, who could not manage everyday life, soon married another man.

In contrast, the honest Fa had worked hard to become wealthy. In the end, he built a house, got married, and became a very different man than his depraved brother.

26 ■ The Yellow Bag

Once there was a very poor and foolish young man. He was so poor that he could barely eat two meals a day. All of his relatives looked down upon him. Consequently, he had to beg in the village, but still could not get enough to eat. Therefore, he went to other towns to beg, and when winter arrived, he begged two bowls of food, but ate only one. Then, he went to a temple for the Earth God near the seashore and lay down on the altar. After crossing his legs and facing the sunshine, he began to sing and banged a broken wok like a gong. The more he sang, the happier he became. His singing got louder and longer, even better than the Chinese *hwamei* bird in the mountains.

"Who is singing at the seashore today?" the Dragon King in the crystal palace asked his guards. "The singing is not bad. Why don't you go up and find out who that is?"

The guards went to the seashore and looked around, but did not see anyone there. Then they went to the temple for the Earth God, looked inside, and saw the beggar in shabby clothes.

"Little beggar! Is it you who's been singing here all the time?" they asked.

"Yes. It is me."

"Our Dragon King would like to hear you singing. Follow us to the deep sea. There is enough to eat and drink there."

"Deep sea? I will be drowned to death!"

"No. Just close your eyes and lay on my shoulder," said one of the guards. "When I set you down, you can open your eyes."

"All right, I'll go if I have food to eat."

He then closed his eyes and lay on the guard's shoulder. Within seconds, he was deposited on the ground beneath the ocean. When he opened his eyes, he saw a shining palace with golden tiles. The Dragon King was sitting on his throne and asked, "Little beggar! Is it you who sings here all the time?"

"Yes. It is me."

"Did you use a little drum while singing?"

"How could I have a drum? I was banging a broken wok," he answered and raised the wok.

"What were you singing?"

"I was singing about plowing and tilling, tilling and plowing. I sing whatever makes me feel happy."

"Now sing something for me."

The young man leaned against the door, banging the broken wok, and was ready to sing.

"How about giving you a red drum?" the Dragon King asked. "Would it sound better?"

"I don't want a drum. That will not match my way of singing."

Once he began singing, the Dragon King said, "Very good, indeed. But your voice is a little low."

"That's because I haven't eaten yet," replied the young man.

The Dragon King immediately ordered his people to serve warm rice wine and hot dishes along with many other things to eat. After eating, the young man tapped his puffed belly and sang with high and low voices. The Dragon King was fascinated and stroked his beard while smiling.

After singing, the young man said, "Now I'd like to return to the town."

The Dragon King liked his singing so much, however, that he wanted to keep him for a longer time.

Ten days passed by quickly. The young man really wanted to go back home, and fortunately, the guard who brought him there told him secretly, "When you leave, the Dragon King will give you something. Don't accept anything except the yellow bag tied to his robe. When you shake the yellow bag, you will have whatever you want."

The young man went to the Dragon King, and said, "Dragon King! I want to go back home."

"Do you have a wife at home? How come you miss your home so much?"

"No, I don't have a wife. But I still miss home."

"Since you want to leave, I would like to give you some gems."

"I don't want gems."

"You don't want gems? What do you want?"

"I'd like only the yellow bag tied to your robe."

The Dragon King thought for a moment and said, "Well, since you want it so much, then I will give it to you!"

He untied the yellow bag and gave it to the young man, who smiled from ear to ear. The same guard again asked him to close his eyes and brought him back to the seashore.

Now, the young man looked at the yellow bag and wondered, "Will this bag really bring me whatever I want? I should give it a try." Therefore, he shook the yellow bag and said, "Oh, how hungry I am! I want to drink some warm rice wine and eat some hot dishes."

Almost immediately, warm rice wine and hot dishes arose out of the yellow bag, and the young man was very glad and said, "Really! I am really lucky!" After he finished eating, he shook the yellow bag again, and said, "My legs are tired now. I want to have a white donkey to ride on."

Immediately, a little white donkey appeared out of the yellow bag. When the villagers saw a beggar on a donkey, they all laughed. Once they recognized that it was the young man, they said, "Little foolish man, where did you steal the donkey?"

"I asked for it," he replied.

"Where is this person?"

"It's not a person who gives me what I want," said the young man, raising his yellow bag. "I get whatever I ask for from this bag."

The villagers did not believe him, and so, the young man said, "Let me invite you all to a feast!"

Immediately, he asked the yellow bag for a feast of dozens of tables filled with warm rice wine and hot dishes. They all ate so much that they fell on the ground and could not stand up.

When the young man got back to his own little rickety shack, he asked for food from the yellow bag every day. He ate so well that he even gained a tremendous amount of weight. One day, he said to himself, "How about I ask for a woman and see if I can get one?"

So, he shook the yellow bag and said, "I want a beautiful woman to warm my feet."

All of a sudden, a beautiful woman popped out of the yellow bag. Indeed, she smiled charmingly at the young man, and he grabbed her hand and felt extremely happy.

Now, the young man had a cousin who came to him one day and said, "Can you lend me the bag so I can play with it for a couple of days?"

"Of course, yes," said the young man, and he gave it to his cousin.

After his cousin got rich, the young man asked him to return the yellow bag, but his cousin refused. The young man got angry and went to the governor to sue his cousin. However, his cousin had made a great deal of money with the yellow bag in the meantime, while the young man lost a lot of money each day. Soon he used up all his money, and without money, how could he start a lawsuit?

One day, the young man said to the woman who had become his wife, "We are in trouble now. Nothing to eat. Nothing to drink."

"You are the one to be blamed," said the woman.

The young man looked at their little dog that had become thinner, and he said, "My doggy, I have nothing to eat, and you are also starving."

The dog heard his words and decided to steal the yellow bag and restore it to his master. So, at night, he ran to the cousin's place and saw an old cat coming out of the house. All at once, he jumped on the cat and pushed it down under his paws. The cat was trembling and scared and said, "Brother Dog, Brother Dog! Are you going to eat me up?"

"I won't eat you up, but you must steal the yellow bag for me from your master," said the dog.

"It is locked in the master's small chest, and the small chest is locked in the big chest. I cannot. . . . Ouch!" The dog pushed and squeezed the cat.

"I will find the rat and ask him to do the job," said the cat.

The dog lifted his paws, and the cat dashed away.

Now there was a big rat at the corner of the house celebrating his birthday. Dozens of small rats were kneeling down on both sides of him and flattering him. Suddenly, the cat jumped into the party and caught one small rat, and bit its ears. The small rat screamed, and the rest ran away except for the big rat, who sat there calmly, looking at the cat, and said, "Uncle Cat, are you going to devour the little rat?"

The old cat shook its head and said, "No, no, no. All you have to do is to go quickly to my master's room and steal the yellow bag out of the small chest. The small chest is inside the big chest. Once you bring the yellow bag to me, I'll let him go."

"Easily done."

The big rat led his tiny rats to the master's room. They bit through the big chest and rolled inside. Then they bit through the small chest, and rolled inside. Once the big rat held the yellow bag in its mouth, he brought it to the old cat. The old cat let go of the small rat underneath his paws, brought the bag outside the house, and gave it to the little dog.

The little dog brought the yellow bag to the young man's room and saw him sitting in the lamplight and murmuring, "Alas, bad luck. . . ."

The little dog rubbed his head on the young man's leg, but the young man said, "Doggy, I have nothing to eat. Are you hungry?"

He reached down his hand to rub the dog's head. Suddenly, he saw the yellow bag in the dog's mouth. He was thrilled and jumped up! "Fantastic! Did you steal this yellow bag for me?"

The young man quickly asked for a lot of warm rice wine and hot dishes. Then he summoned his wife, and they all ate together—the young man, the dog, and his wife.

The next day, the young man went to the court again to sue his cousin. Now with the yellow bag, he had tons more money. Since his cousin no longer had the bag, he lost the lawsuit and all his money as well.

Once there were two sisters. The elder sister was very beautiful, but the younger sister was even more beautiful. After the elder sister got married, her husband would keep her company at home every day and did not want to do any business outside the house. One day, the elder sister cautioned him and said, "Why do you stare at me from morning till night? Don't you see I am the same person all the time?"

"You are so beautiful, so exquisitely beautiful. How can I be away from you even for one second?" her husband replied.

"You think I am beautiful? My younger sister at home is the real beautiful one!"

"Then can I invite her to our home so I can have a look at her?"

"No, I don't want you to invite her here. If you do, I'll hang myself!"

"Is she so formal? Then I must try to get her here!" said the husband.

In the old days, women were careful about the formalities, and younger sisters would rarely visit their brother-in-law's house. So, her elder sister's husband thought of a strategy to entice the younger sister.

A few days later, he sent someone to his mother-in-law's house with a message:

"Your elder sister is seriously ill. She seems to be as hot as fire at daytime, but as cold as ice at nighttime. She wants to see her younger sister before she dies."

The younger sister believed the messenger and immediately traveled by sedan to her brother-in-law's house. When the two sisters met, the younger realized it was all nonsense: the elder sister was not sick at all!

The brother-in-law saw that his sister-in-law was indeed unusually beautiful. His wife was a grade lower in comparison. Then he said to his wife, "Look! You said that I couldn't and shouldn't get her here!"

But she said nothing. A moment later, she walked to her own room and tied a rope around her neck. Then she hanged herself.

Her husband took care of her funeral and then went to his mother-in-law to ask for the younger sister's hand in marriage. The mother-in-law had liked him as a son-in-law from the beginning. Now, after he used flattering and duplicitous words, she agreed to let him marry the younger sister.

After they were married, they fell deeply in love. But the soul of the elder sister was transformed into a bird and hid in a tree in front of their bedroom window. Whenever the younger sister combed her hair, the bird would cry out, "Sis *chiu-ke-chiu*! Using my comb to comb a dog head! Sis *chiu-ke-chiu*! Using my flower to show my man!"

And the bird uttered cries like this every day. The younger sister became extremely angry, until finally she picked up a stick and threw it at the bird and killed it. She plucked all the feathers from the bird and then cooked it. When she ate the bird, there were nothing but bones, and when her husband ate, it was all meat. They switched plates but the same thing still happened. The younger sister was very angry again and poured the remaining parts in the pot outside the window in the middle of the yard.

Before long, a bamboo shoot sprouted in the courtyard. After the bamboo grew bigger, the younger sister asked a weaver to make a carriage. But when she put her children into the carriage, they all died one by one. She became so angry again that she broke the carriage and then burned it. As the fire was burning, a poisonous snake emerged and coiled itself around the neck of the younger sister and squeezed her to death.

28 ■ The Elder Daughter

Once upon a time, there was a farmer who had two wives. The first wife gave birth to a daughter and then died. The second wife also gave birth to a daughter. Before long, the farmer died. All the family properties were left to the second wife and two daughters.

The second wife was not kind-hearted. She realized that the elder daughter was not her own, but was very beautiful; the younger daughter was her own, but her face was full of pockmarks. Consequently, she was very mean and cruel to the elder daughter.

One day, she took the younger daughter to visit her mother. Before she left, she mixed some buckwheat hulls, wheat, and mung beans together and said to the elder daughter, "Guard the house. Separate the buckwheat hulls, wheat, and mung beans in the sieve. Don't be lazy. If you don't get the job done, I'll give you a good beating."

The elder daughter looked at the mixed buckwheat hulls, wheat, and mung beans in the big sieve. How could she separate them?

"Oh, my dear mother!" she couldn't stop herself from crying. "How can I separate all this in the sieve? My dear mother!"

民間故事之二

鳥的故事

林蒲編

Y.N.

Then a crow appeared and landed on the roof, and called out loudly.

"Don't cry, my dear daughter!" the crow exclaimed. "Bring out the sieves and sifters!"

Therefore, the elder daughter took out many sieves and sifters and put them on the ground. Soon, many crows, magpies, and sparrows arrived. They covered the whole yard. In less than half a day, all the buckwheat hulls, wheat, and mung beans were separated.

When her stepmother returned, she was pleased that the job had been done without any difficulty. Therefore, the next day, she asked the elder daughter to herd a cow in the mountains.

"Don't come back for food," she said, "until you can feed the cow so well that it will spurt gold from its behind."

The elder daughter took the cow to the mountains, but the cow did not lay any gold. As the sun was about to set, she sat at a grave and cried, "My dear mother. I was asked to herd the cow until it lays gold. If the cow fails, I can't go back home. Oh, my dear mother, what should I do?"

Then a crow flew and landed on a tree. "Don't cry, my dear daughter," the crow said. "Go to the cow, and wait until it spurts gold!"

The elder daughter quickly pulled up her skirt flap and waited at the cow's behind. Soon, the cow lifted its tail and laid a lot of gold.

The third day, her stepmother did not ask her to herd the cow. Instead, she asked the younger daughter to dress up with her new clothes and take the cow to the mountains. Before her daughter left, she told her to do what the elder daughter had done the day earlier.

When it became dark, the younger daughter sat at a grave and cried, "Oh, my dear mother. You asked me to herd the cow until it lays gold. You told me I can't return home until I have the gold. Oh, my dear mother, what should I do?"

All of a sudden, a crow landed on a tree and shouted, "Don't cry, younger daughter. Go to the cow and wait until it spurts gold."

She quickly pulled up her skirt and waited at the cow's behind. The cow lifted its tail, and all at once it lay a huge pile of dung on her lap.

29 ■ The Three Brothers

Once upon a time, there were three brothers who did not get along well with one another. Therefore, they divided their possessions and animals. The eldest brother got the mule and the horse. The second brother got the donkey and the cow. The third brother, Xiao San (Little Three), got the cat and the dog.

Afterward, Xiao San took his cat and dog to help him plow in the field. As he was working, a rich man came by on horseback. He was surprised by what he saw and said, "I have seen a mule and a horse plowing in the field, but I've never seen a cat and a dog plowing in the field."

"Don't look down upon my cat, and don't look down upon my dog," Xiao San replied. "One stroke with the whip on my cat and dog, and they will search anywhere for me. One stroke with the stick, and they will go anywhere for me. One strike with the awl, and they will fly anywhere."

The rich man said, "I don't believe you. I'll bet my horse that this isn't true."

Xiao San then demonstrated to him. Indeed, with one stroke, the cat and the dog took off, searched, and flew everywhere. So, the rich man lost his horse. Then, Xiao San led the horse home along with his cat and dog.

When his two brothers saw this, they asked, "Xiao San! Where did you get the horse?"

Xiao San told them the truth. Since the second brother was very jealous, he went to Xiao San's house the next day and said, "Why don't you lend me your cat and dog?"

Xiao San was very honest, and so he lent his cat and dog to his second brother, who took the cat and dog to plow in the field. Soon another rich man passed by on horseback.

The rich man was very surprised and said, "I have seen a mule and a horse plowing in the field, but I've never seen the cat and the dog plowing in the field."

"Don't look down upon my cat. Don't look down upon my dog," said the second brother, following Xiao San's words. "One stroke with the whip on my cat and dog, and they will search everywhere for me. One stroke with the stick, and they will go anywhere. One stroke with the awl, and they will fly everywhere."

The rich man said, "I don't believe you. I'll bet my horse that this isn't true."

The second brother demonstrated everything to him. However, no matter how hard he struck the cat and the dog, they would not move at all. He was very angry and cursed, "Damn! You are cheating me!"

He then became violent and killed the cat and the dog with the plow and went home.

Xiao San did not see his cat and dog returning home. So, he went to his second brother's house, who said with anger and remorse, "I beat the cat and dog to death and threw their bodies into the end of the field."

When Xiao San heard this, he became very sad, rushed to the field, and buried the cat and dog there. Afterward, he planted a tree on top of the tomb.

The tree grew bigger and bigger, and on the anniversary day of the death of the cat and dog, Xiao San bought some peaches and a bottle of wine. He put them on a plate as sacrifices. Then he went up to the tomb and prayed, "Oh, my cat, come out and eat the peaches! Oh, my dog, come out and drink the wine!"

As he was praying, a sudden gust of wind blew his cap up to the treetop. Xiao San tried to shake the tree, and many coins fell off the tree. Quickly, he picked them up, put them all on the plate, and carried the plate full of money back home.

The second brother saw him again and said, "Xiao San, where did you steal the silver?"

Xiao San replied, "I didn't steal these silver coins."

He then told his second brother how he had offered sacrifices to the cat and dog.

His eldest brother heard him and said, "Really? Then I want to make an offering as well."

The next day, he bought some peaches, filled a bottle with wine, and put them on a plate. Then he went to the tree, set out the peaches and wine as offerings, and began to pray, "Oh, my cat, come out to eat the peaches! Oh my dog, come out and drink the wine!"

He shouted for a long time, but there was no wind at all. Consequently, he became so upset that he threw his cap up onto the tree. Next, he began to shake the tree, but many dog poops fell on his head. Now he became so angry that he chopped down the tree. After he cut the tree, the three brothers divided the tree. The eldest brother got the tree trunk. The second brother got the branches.

Xiao San got the twigs and used them and small branches to weave a big basket. One day, he carried the basket on his back and came to a temple. At the temple gate, he set the basket down under the eaves, spread some millet stalks on top of the basket, and shouted, "Swallows from the east! Swallows from the west! Eat the millet and lay some eggs." Indeed, many swallows came. They did not eat any millet, but each laid an egg. Soon, the basket was filled with eggs, and Xiao San then carried the basket home.

The second brother saw him again and asked, "Xiao San, where did you get those eggs?" Xiao San told him everything.

"Really? Then I would like to try it," the second brother said.

He then carried the basket on his back and took a small bag of millet stalks and left. When he got to the temple gate, he spread the millet on the basket and put it under the eaves. Then, he shouted, "Swallows from the east! Swallows from the west! Eat the millet and lay some eggs."

As he was shouting, a flock of swallows arrived. They ate the millet and lay poops, and soon the basket was full of bird poops. He was so angry that he burned the basket in the stove.

Xiao San asked for his basket, but his eldest brother told him it was burned. Xiao San then used a stick to try to dig out the basket from the stove. As he was digging, some sweet peas popped from the ground. Xiao San took a bite and found they were very delicious. He ate all the sweet peas and felt his whole body was delicious. He then ran into the street and shouted, "So delicious! So fragrant! Who would like to take me to scent their clothes?"

As he was shouting, an official appeared and asked, "Really that fragrant? Come and make my clothes fragrant!"

Xiao San went and lay down in a big closet. Soon, the whole closet smelled very delicious and fragrant. The official awarded him with a lot of money.

The second brother saw the money and asked, "Xiao San, where did you steal the silver coins from?"

Xiao San said, "I didn't steal the silver. I earned it."

He then told the whole story, and the second brother said, "Really? I would like to try it."

Therefore, he went to the stove to dig, but there was not even one pea. Then he had an idea. He grabbed a handful of black beans and threw them into the stove. When they were cooked, he ate them all. Then he ran to the street, and shouted, "So delicious! So fragrant! Who would like to take me to scent their clothes?"

As he was shouting, an official arrived and asked, "Really that fragrant? Come and make my clothes fragrant!"

The second brother followed the official to his house, and they locked him in a big closet. After a long time, they asked him to get out. He laid many poops in the closet and made all the clothes dirty because he ate too many beans. The official was so angry that he ordered his men to beat him, and they even stuck a wooden chock up his asshole.

30 ■ Elder Brother and Younger Brother

Once upon a time, there were two brothers. The elder brother was called Li Da (Big), and the younger Li Xi (Thin). They were very poor, had very little food, and their clothes and hut were in bad shape. In addition, they lived with their widowed mother.

One day, the mother said to the two brothers, "Alas, we are so poor. If we don't figure out a way to make our living, we are going to die a wretched death. I am already too old, and I don't want to live in this world any longer. However, you must have plans for your future. You are young, and you should do something great so that you fulfill your life as strong men! Look at our neighbor, the Chen family. How rich they are! They have horse carriages they use when they go out, and they have servants who wait on them. They have had good fortune in this life! But they struggled hard when they were young. Now I only hope you can . . ."

She could not finish her words, as tears were pouring out like fountains. She cried, and the two brothers cried too. After a while, Li Da said, "Mother, we have also been hoping to do something great in life. But, as they say, 'you need a handful of rice to steal a chicken.' We don't even have one copper penny. We have nothing. Even if we work hard, there is nothing there to help us. Mother, don't cry. We must think of a solution. Perhaps our neighbors, the Chens, who are so rich, can lend us ten dollars. For them, this money does not mean anything. If they lend us this money, we can give you two dollars as food money for a little while. Then we will spend two dollars for our fare. We can then use the remaining six dollars to start a business. Do you think this is possible? Mother, what do you think?"

"That sounds good," their mother smiled at this idea and said, "I will go then to see if we can borrow that money."

After the three agreed, the mother went to the Chens. Indeed, she got the loan. However, the younger brother Li Xi was not kind-hearted at all. When he saw the money, he had a bad idea.

A day later, they followed their plan and left two dollars for their mother as food money. Then, they changed the remaining eight dollars to eight hundred pennies. They put the money in a bag, packed their luggage, and were ready for the departure the following morning.

The next day, the younger brother carried the luggage, and the elder brother carried the money bag. Just about three or four miles after they had departed, the younger brother said, "Elder brother, your money bag is so heavy that your shoulders must be tired. Let's switch."

"Younger brother, you are also carrying the luggage on your shoulders. No need. I am all right with it," the elder brother replied.

"Your money bag is much heavier than the luggage! Your shoulders must be sore now. Let's switch!"

"Younger brother, you are so kind," said the elder brother, not knowing his brother had an evil idea in mind. "All right, let's switch," he continued.

Therefore, they switched bags and walked for another three or four miles. The younger brother pretended that he had a stomachache, and said, "My stomach hurts. Let me rest here for a while. You can go ahead, and I will catch up with you after I rest a bit. Is that all right?"

"That's not good," said the elder brother. "We have the same journey, though not the same fate. We should take care of each other when one of us is sick. How can I go ahead without you?"

"Elder brother, since you are so concerned, would you please put down your bags and find a family nearby and get some hot soup for me?" the younger brother asked.

When the elder brother heard this, he put down his bag and walked to a village to find some hot water. He was thinking hard as he walked. You ask what he was thinking about. Well, he was thinking, "What will I do if my younger brother dies?"

He kept walking, without knowing how far he went. Then he saw an old woman working in the field. He walked up to her and asked for a cup of tea to bring back to his younger brother. But, when he went back to the place, he could not find his younger brother. He didn't realize that his younger brother had already taken the money and had run away. Instead, he thought for a while and guessed that his younger brother must have gone ahead while he was not there. Why else wasn't he there?

The elder brother then poured the cup of tea on the ground and walked onward aimlessly. Now the sun began to set, and there was a crescent moon on the edge of the sky. He became more and more anxious as he walked. Suddenly, he saw a pavilion in the distance. He was tired, and wanted to spend the night there. This pavilion was called the Traveling Immortal Pavilion.

There was an attic in the pavilion, but he thought it was not good to sleep up there. Therefore, he lay down on a stone bench to sleep.

Just as he fell asleep, he suddenly heard a few people talking. Since this was the Traveling Immortal Pavilion and was for traveling immortals, there were some immortals gathering here on the fifteenth day of the eighth moon every year. It turned out that those immortals were talking, and one of them said, "We have nothing to do, and no wine and dishes to enjoy. So boring."

"I have a stick here. If you knock at it once, you can get the wine and dishes you want," another immortal said.

A moment later, there was a sound of a stick knocking, and someone said, "Look, there are now wine and dishes on the table."

Then there were sounds of drinking and eating while the immortals were chatting and laughing. One voice said, "There is a Bitter Water Spring in the east, and the people in that region don't have good water to drink. Is there a way to change the bitter water to normal water?"

"That is very easy," an old man said. "If the pine tree next to the spring is removed and the dark snake beneath it is killed, then the water from that spring will become normal."

"There is a bridge in the west," a young man joined the conversation. "They started building it twelve years ago, but it is still not completed. Is there a way to successfully complete it?"

"Do you know why they haven't finished building it?" a loud voice commented. "Because there are four jars of gold and four jars of silver underneath the bridge. If these jars are removed, that bridge will be successfully completed."

A moment later, all the clinking sounds of cups, dishes, bowls, chopsticks, spoons, and talking and laughing gradually disappeared, and the sound of heavy steps faded away. Soon, the sun began rising. There were birds chirping on trees. The elder brother got up and walked out of the pavilion and felt hungry. Suddenly, he saw a stick next to the stone table. He recalled the scene he saw in his dream and quickly picked it up. Then he began knocking and talking to it. Very soon, the table was filled with wine and dishes. He rushed to eat and drink and then started to think of his younger brother. He did not know where his young brother was, and felt sorry not to be able to eat together with him.

After eating, he picked up the stick and walked toward the east. After a long while, he saw an old woman fetching water. Since he felt thirsty after walking for such a long time, he walked up to the woman and said, "Auntie, I have walked for a long time and am very thirsty. Could you give me a little water to drink?"

"The water here is very bitter. So, you must cook the water," the old woman said.

He heard these words and remembered the conversation he heard in the dream. Then he hastened to ask, "Is this spring called Bitter Water Spring?"

"Yes! Yes!"

"Then I can tell you people a way to change this bitter water into normal water. Is that all right?"

"Can you? That would be wonderful!"

"There is a pine tree next to the spring, and there is a dark snake underneath the tree. If the tree is dug up, and the snake is killed, then the water will be normal."

After he said this, he wanted to depart, but the woman stopped him and asked for his name and where his home was. Therefore, he told her everything.

Then he walked toward the west, and about two or three miles away, he saw many people building a bridge. He then remembered the conversation he heard in his dream. So, he asked those people, "How long have you been building this bridge?"

"Already twelve years," they replied.

"Oh, such a long time. How come you have not completed it?" he asked.

"Alas! Indeed, it's been a long time. Whenever we finish building the bridge, it collapses. So we have never successfully completed it."

"I can tell you a way to get the work done," he said.

"You know how to get the work done? That is great!" they said.

He then told the people, "The reason that this bridge can never be completed is that there are four jars of gold and four jars of silver underneath the foundation. If they are dug out, then you can successfully complete the bridge."

Those workers were very happy, and they thanked him and asked his name and where he came from. He told them everything they asked and then departed.

Once he returned home, his mother asked, "You and your brother went out to find work. Did you make any money?"

His tears ran down his cheeks. He told his mother what happened on their way out: how he spent the night at the Traveling Immortal Pavilion, what happened next, everything that had happened. His mother heard those words, and cried, "So, your younger brother will not return home!"

"Well, I don't know where he went," he said.

Two months passed, and they lived well thanks to the magic stick.

One day, the emperor heard that the Bitter Water Spring in the east now had normal water and that the bridge in the west was finally completed, and that it was Li Da who told the people how to get those things done. Therefore, the emperor sent many ministers who brought lots of gems and gold and silver to Li Da's house. People from the east brought a lot of gold and silver to him as well. People from the west brought four jars of gold and four jars of silver to him. Li Da now became a rich man. He built a new house and married a wife. From then on, he enjoyed a wonderful life!

One day, his younger brother passed by his gate just as the elder brother came out of the house. He saw a beggar. It was his younger brother! Therefore, he called to his younger brother and gave him new clothes and treated him with wine and dishes.

"Elder brother, you must have made a fortune from your business these years," the younger brother said.

"I did not make a fortune in doing business," he replied. Then he told his younger brother everything that happened after they separated.

The younger brother heard all this and thought that he would do well by doing just what his elder brother did at the pavilion. Therefore, when it turned dark, he ran to the Traveling Immortal Pavilion, climbed up to the attic, and got ready to sleep in it. Suddenly, he heard some immortals talking underneath, and he felt excited.

Soon he heard one immortal say, "When we had our gathering the other year, I left my stick here. Who took it?"

"There must be a thief here. A thief must have stolen the stick. Let me go up and see if there is a thief there," said one immortal who then climbed up to the attic. All at once, he saw a man sleeping there.

"Look! The stick must have been stolen by this thief," said one immortal.

Without asking anything, they picked up the man and began to beat him up. They pulled his nose until it was twelve feet long and then let the man run away. So, the younger brother ran home and told everything to his elder brother.

"Don't worry. Everything will be all right. If they want the stick, I will bring it back to them. Let's also find a way to fix your nose," the elder brother said.

In the evening, the elder brother ran to the Traveling Immortal Pavilion and climbed up to the attic. A moment later, he heard a few immortals talking about what had happened the night before. One immortal said, "How funny it was! I pulled the man's nose that long!"

Another immortal said, "Is there a way to cure him?"

"That's easy," the first immortal said. "You just have to take the stick and hit him once, and call his name once, and he must answer once. If you use the stick like that twelve times, his nose will turn back to normal."

The elder brother heard that and learned it by heart. At daybreak, he rushed home and said to his brother, "Younger brother! There is a way to cure your nose. I'll use the stick to hit you once and call you once, and you are to answer once. If we do that twelve times, your nose will return to normal."

Therefore, the elder brother hit him with the stick twelve times, called his younger brother's name twelve times, and his younger brother answered twelve times. Who knew why the younger brother continued, "Not enough! Not enough! One more time! One more time!"

The elder brother then hit him one more time. Wow! The younger brother's nose suddenly became flat!

31 ■ The Melon King

Once upon a time, two brothers divided their household property. Gege (elder brother) was mean and cruel. He took the good farming land as his share and gave the bad land on the hill to Didi (younger brother), who was too young and did not understand the way of the world, but just listened to Gege.

Since Didi had the bad land on the hill, he could not grow rice. Instead, he grew melons. Unexpectedly, before the melons turned ripe, they were all picked by the monkeys from the mountains. Once that occurred, not a single melon was left. Didi was very upset and wanted to find a way to keep the monkeys away so that they would never come again. Consequently, he thought for days and nights, and finally he had a clever plan. He took a kitchen cleaver and a small gong and put himself in a cloth bag hanging on the shed next to the melon field. He thought, "When the monkeys come, I'll bang the gong to scare them away. If they do not flee, I'll use the knife to cut open the bag and jump out and kill all the monkeys one by one. Not a single monkey will be left. That will be my revenge."

However, he waited in the bag for a long time, but the monkeys did not arrive. Now, it was deep in the night, and he was tired and could not help falling asleep in the bag. As soon as he slept, the monkeys came. They saw a bag hanging up there on the shed and felt very happy, because they thought it was a huge melon.

"Wow, such a big melon!" they said to one another. "Never seen one like this. Must be a melon king."

Then they took down the bag and carried it home. On the way, Didi woke up from a scary dream. He looked outside from a small hole in the bag. He saw more than ten monkeys carrying him walking in the moonlight. He was so scared that he dared not even bang the gong in his hands and just kept quiet inside the bag.

When he was carried into a cave, the day began to break. The monkeys put him on a piece of high and flat rock. He thought it must be the monkeys' dinner table, because there were also small square rocks around like stools. Then all the monkeys bowed in front of him. He thought that it might be a ritual that the monkeys performed before they ate the melons. Just at this moment, he decided to bang the gong loudly—Dang! Dang! Dang! All the monkeys ran out of the cave with great fear.

Didi came out of the bag and looked around. He saw that there were not only many melons and fruits, but also a lot of jewels and treasures. He was thrilled, and filled the bag with jewels and treasures, carried everything home, and became a rich person.

Gege heard of this and was impressed. So, he went to ask Didi to exchange their land. Didi readily agreed. Gege now had the land on the hill and copied what his younger brother did. However, when the monkeys carried him over a bridge, he could not hold his pee and poop. Then all the pee and poop came out of the bag and fell on the monkeys. They smelled the stinky stuff and said, "Terrible! This melon king must be rotten and is no longer edible."

Suddenly, they stopped and dumped the bag into the river, where it made a big splash.

PART FOUR

Other Odd Tales

Once there was an old woman who had ten sons. The first son was called Long Spirit, the second Fly Leg, the third Iron Neck, the fourth Loose Skin, the fifth Thick Leg, the sixth Big Head, the seventh Long Leg, the eighth Big Nose, the ninth Water Eye, and the tenth Pout Lip.

At that time, there was an emperor who wanted to build the Five Phoenix Building, but three years passed, and he could not get it done. Finally, the emperor issued an edict, "Whoever can build it in three months will be promoted to a high rank."

The first brother, Long Spirit, went to the emperor, and he finished the job in three days. He built the Five Phoenix Building high up to the sky with five phoenixes on the roof as if flying. The emperor said, "How capable he is! If I don't kill him, he will eventually rebel."

So, Long Spirit was bound and sent to the execution site. Meanwhile, the second brother, Fly Leg, carried the third brother, Iron Neck, on his back to the site. They lived more than ten miles from the execution site, but he ran there in one breath.

When they arrived, Iron Neck said, "Kill me, please! Kill me, please! I am so skinny and can't do anything, but my big brother has strength and can beg food for our mother."

Thanks to Iron Neck's pleas, Long Spirit was released. Then, two executioners raised their big knives and were ready to kill Iron Neck. When the first knife chopped on his neck, there were only sparks, and the blade of the knife was broken. The second knife managed to hit his neck, but the blade clanked and fell apart. The executioners struck repeatedly, but they were unable to cut off the head. Consequently, the emperor cried out, "Since the blade can't kill him, he will be replaced by Loose Skin!"

Fly Leg heard that they would execute Loose Skin instead of Iron Neck. So, he hurried back and carried the fourth brother, Loose Skin, on his back to the site.

When he arrived, Loose Skin shouted, "Pull me! Pull me! I am a useless person and have loose skin all over my body."

So, Iron Neck was released. Now, Loose Skin had one cow tied to his head, one cow to his left hand, one cow to his right hand, one cow to his left foot, and one cow to his right foot. There were five whips for the five cows, and they were all whipped at the same time. The five cows pulled as hard as they could. Loose Skin's head skin was pulled a few miles long. The skin of his hands was also pulled a few miles long. However, he did not die at all. He just gazed at the sky.

Once again, the emperor was angry and cried out: "Since we can't kill Loose Skin, bring their entire family here and kill them all!"

When Fly Leg heard that his whole family would be killed, he carried Loose Skin back home on his back, shouting from far away, "The emperor wants to kill the whole family! Everyone run away quickly!"

Well before the emperor's guards had arrived, the family had run away. They ran and ran, until they came to a big river with huge waves. The seventh brother, Long Leg, said, "Let me walk in and see how deep it is."

So, he walked into the river. It was several dozen yards deep, but it was only up to his leg calf. Therefore, he carried the whole family across the river.

Now, they were hungry. What to do? Long Leg said, "Let me catch a few fish in the river."

Within seconds, he caught two big fish. Then, he asked his mother to cut open the fish's stomach. When she cut open one fish, out came a boat with thirteen sails. She cut open the other fish, and out came another boat with thirteen sails. There were also many people on the boats. They all thanked her, and said, "Thank you for your cutting open the fish's stomach. Otherwise, we thought we would never see the sky again."

The two boats sailed downstream, and the people on the boats gave two rolls of red silk to her to make clothes. The two fish were put in a pot they brought with them, but there was no firewood. What to do? The fifth brother, Thick Leg, said, "There are still two splinters in my legs. Pull them out, and there should be enough wood."

They pulled out two thick logs and cut them into two bundles. The others were resting aside, and only the eighth brother, Big Nose, was blowing the fire. Soon, the smell of the cooked fish reached his nose and caused him to drool. He lifted the pot cover, and smelled with his nose. The two fish were sucked into his stomach by his nose. The sixth brother, Big Head, frowned and wanted to hit Big Nose. However, their mother said, "Don't be upset. I will not make clothes with these two rolls of red silk. I'll make a hat for you."

She quickly made a hat with the two rolls of silk, but it could not even cover his head top. He was upset and threw the hat on the ground. The ninth brother, Water Eye, was sleeping. The hat touched his eyes, and water flowed out of his eyes. It formed a flood that covered only nine counties and twelve districts. The tenth brother, Pout Lip, looked around, and said, "This is really going too far! Wow!"

He pouted his lips and blew open the South Heaven Gate!

民間童話集之一

換心後

林蘭編

1930

Y.N.

Once there was a young girl who lost her mother. When her father remarried, she often suffered from her stepmother's scolding and beating, and from time to time was not given food to eat. She felt that she had no place to pour out her bitter feelings. She could only run to her mother's grave and cry there. Her tears flooded the earth, and suddenly, a stalk of rice with two ears grew from the spot where her tears dropped. She was so hungry that she picked the two ears of rice, twisted off the hulls, and put the rice into her mouth. To her surprise, after eating the rice, her stomach began to get bigger and bigger. When she returned home with a big stomach, her stepmother assumed that she must have become pregnant, and thus she treated her even worse. When it was about midnight, the girl gave birth to three babies. Strangely enough, the three babies grew quickly after a wind whisked by. Very soon, they grew up and became strong young men. They took turns carrying their mother on their backs and traveled to an ancient cave in the mountains, where the three sons went hunting every day.

Once, when they were out hunting, several robbers passed the cave and saw the unusually beautiful young girl.

"Hey, little girl," they said to her, "come with us, and we'll make sure you will have enough to eat and drink."

"No. I don't want to go with you," the girl replied. "I have three sons, and I'd prefer to remain here."

"If you don't go with us," the robbers cried, "our knives are not going to be polite with you."

Since the girl kept saying no, one of the robbers raised his knife and chopped her head off. Then, when the three sons came back and saw their mother dead, they put her head and body together, and she was suddenly alive again.

A few days later, the robbers passed the cave again. When they saw the girl, they said, "Hey, little girl. How come you are alive again?"

"My sons put my head and body together, that's why I'm alive again," she said.

"You'd better come with us. We'll make sure you have enough to eat and drink," they said.

The girl kept saying no. Therefore, the robbers chopped her into eight pieces, and said, "Let's see what your sons can do about this now."

The three sons came back and saw that their mother was chopped into eight pieces. Once they put her limbs and body together, she became alive.

A few days later, the robbers passed the cave again. Once they saw the girl, they said, "Hey, little girl. How come you are alive again?"

"My sons put my limbs and body together, and this is why I am alive again," she said.

"You'd better come with us. You'll have enough to eat and drink," they said.

The girl kept saying no. As a result, the robbers pulled out their steel knives and chopped her into ten pieces. As they left, they took a leg with them and said, "Let's see what your sons can do about this now."

The three sons came back and saw that their mother was chopped into ten pieces. Therefore, they put her limbs and body together, and she became alive, missing one leg. As they were trying to think of a way out of this situation, they saw a messenger coming from the south. So, they cut off the messenger's leg and attached it to their mother's body. But now, they asked themselves, how could the messenger travel without one leg? Just at this time, a yellow dog ran out of the woods. So, they cut off the yellow dog's leg, and they attached it to the messenger's body. That is why messengers are now called running dogs.

A few days later, the robbers passed the cave again. When they saw the girl, they said, "Hey, little girl. How come you are alive again?"

"My sons put my limbs and body together, and this is why I am alive again. They borrowed one leg from a messenger."

"You'd better come with us, and we'll give you more than enough to eat and drink," they said.

The girl kept saying no. So, the robbers pulled out their steel knives and cut open her stomach. They took out her heart and put it into one of the robber's pocket, and said, "Let's see what your sons can do about this."

The three sons came back and saw their mother's stomach was cut open. Once they found her heart was missing, they asked themselves whether they'd be able to retrieve it. However, they could only find a dog. Therefore, they took the dog's heart and put it into their mother's chest. Of course, their mother came alive again. Yet, what could they do about the dog without a heart? After conversing a while, they decided to mix a lump of clay and put it into the dog's chest.

A few days later, the robbers passed the cave again. When they saw the girl, they said, "Hey, little girl. How come you are alive again?"

The girl made blurred sounds and could not say a word.

"You'd better come with us," they said. "We'll give you enough to eat and drink," they said.

This time the girl did not put up any resistance and followed them.

34 ■ The Hairy Girl on the Pine Tree

Once there was a Shao family living on the north side of the Yilu Mountain (in Jiangsu Province), and they had a strange tree in their yard. It was green throughout the seasons, and early every morning some pieces of copper would fall off the tree. The copper pieces were round. If a hole was chiseled in the middle, it could be used as money. So, the job of chiseling the holes and stringing the copper pieces was given to the young girl who had been taken into the family as the child-wife of the young boy of the family. She had to get up before daybreak every day to use a chisel and a hammer to do the work nonstop until sunrise in order to finish the job. Then her mother-in-law would get up. She would not let the girl eat, but took her to collect grass on the mountains. The poor girl had calluses all over her hands owing to the hard work of chiseling the copper pieces, and often she had bleeding wounds as well. During the winter, the blood dripping from her hands often filled one or two wine cups.

One cold winter day, she was collecting grass on the mountains dressed only in strips of cloth made from rags. When a gust of wind came, she became so cold that she trembled and coiled together like a worm. She couldn't help thinking about her suffering, and began to cry as she sat on the slope of the mountain. While she was crying, an old man walked out of the pine trees and asked, "Young girl, what are you crying for?"

The child-wife said, "My family has a strange tree. Every early morning many pieces of copper fall off the tree, and my mother-in-law has ordered me to chisel holes in the middle of the pieces to use them as money. This job is very hard for me. My hands bleed so much. . . ."

The old man pointed to the mountain and said, "Do you see that stone human figure? He's pointing one finger at your house and causes those copper pieces to fall off the tree. If you break that finger, the tree will die."

The child-wife bowed several times in gratitude to the old man as he left. Then she collected a full basket of grass that she brought home. She then hid a hammer in her basket. Next, she went to the stone human figure and knocked the finger off with the hammer.

The following day, her mother-in-law saw that the tree had withered. She guessed it was the child-wife who had killed the tree.

"You little demon!" she cursed, "If you don't bring my tree back to life, I'll make you die together with the tree."

The child-wife was so scared that she ran out of the house into the backyard and did not dare to return home. Since it was winter, there was no fruit in the mountains. Consequently, she was so hungry that she had to eat the pine tree. Then strange things happened. After eating the pine tree for a few months, she began to have white hairs grow out of her body, and the hair waved in the air.

There was an immortal pine tree in front of the gate of Loyal Convent Temple. Usually, when the leaves were cut off, new leaves would grow back quickly. However, for several mornings, the old monk saw that half of the leaves had disappeared. He wondered, "What creature would eat these leaves?"

Suspicious, he stayed awake that night and kept looking at the tree from the door. When the moon came out in the middle of the night, he heard the whistling wind of the woods. A strange thing fell off the tree. Its mouth opened and closed, and it kept eating the pine leaves. Its body was covered in white hair, and, in the moonlight, it looked like a white sheep. He wondered, "Who knows if it is a demon or a god?"

The next night, he had a table of meat dishes prepared underneath the pine tree, and the hot steam from the dishes rose above. He thought that if the white hairy creature were a god, it would not eat meat, and if it were a demon, it would devour everything. It was about midnight, and the monk took out his sword. He saw the white hairy thing fall from the sky and land on the immortal pine tree. It smelled with its nose and drooled water from its mouth. It then looked beneath the tree and suddenly flew to the table. It grabbed a fish with one hand and meat with another hand, and began to stuff them into its mouth. Just at this moment, the monk opened the temple gate and raised his sword, shouting, "What demon are you?"

The white hairy creature raised its arms and hands and wanted to fly away, but couldn't. Therefore, it knelt down and said, "I am not a demon. I am the child-wife of the Shao family."

The monk waved his sword and said, "You are the child-wife of the Shao family? Then why are you like this?"

"I killed the strange tree of their family, and my mother-in-law wanted to kill me in return. I was scared and fled. I had nothing to eat but the pine leaves. After eating the pine for two months, white hairs grew from my body, and I could fly. There are not many pine trees on that mountain, and they taste bitter. Only this tree tastes especially good, and it has an endless amount of leaves. I am afraid to be seen during daytime, so I always fly during the night. I have been here more than ten times. This time I saw a table of meat dishes. Master, I have not eaten real food for three months. So, when I saw this delicious food, how could I not crave to eat it? But since I ate fish and meat, I can't fly any more. Master, please forgive me!"

The monk put down his sword and said, "Since you are the child-wife of the Shao family, just stay here now, and I will bring you back home tomorrow."

"I don't want to go back home. My mother-in-law's stick is very frightening," she said.

"Don't be afraid. I will take care of that," said the monk. So, she followed him into the temple.

At daybreak, the monk saw that the child-wife had only a few strips of clothes on her body but no real clothes. Then he found a few pieces of worn clothes for her and brought her home. Once the mother-in-law saw that the child-wife was with the monk, she had to stop beating her. For the next two months, the girl ate real food, and the white hair on her body disappeared completely. In the end, her original looks returned to her.

35 ■ The Shedding Winter Plum

Once there was a girl named Winter Plum. She lost her parents when she was young and was raised by her elder brother and his wife. Her face looked quite ugly—small and pale with big black pockmarks and scabs on her head. She didn't have much hair and was unable to make a braid because it was messy and loose. In short, she looked shabby from head to toe.

One day, her sister-in-law combed her hair and laughed, "Look at your sparse yellow hair! How will you be able to find a husband? Look at you! You can only serve now as a step for mounting a horse!"

Her sister-in-law asked her every day either to feed pigs or to herd cows. But she was very wild and often damaged the neighbors' crops or trees. Others often blamed her sister-in-law, so she made Winter Plum do all the hard jobs such as herding the cows and picking cotton to spin yarn.

Sometimes, however, Winter Plum brought the cotton to the field, and put some on trees here and there. The trees looked like they had white hair and white beards. Then she continued playing, climbing trees, holding the tree branches with her hands, and dangling and swinging her feet. While she was doing all this, she sang:

"Mulberry leaves yellow,

Long leaves of willow,

An empress I shall become."

When she returned home in the evening, all the cotton had been spun into yarn. This astonished many people, who would say that she was cheating. Her sister-in-law thought she still had too much time to play and gave her even more cotton to spin. Every day, she had more and more cotton, but it all became yarn in the evening. Meanwhile, she still played in the field and liked being naughty by tricking people as she did before.

The matchmaker in the imperial court calculated that the future empress had already been born and grown up. So, he sent messengers around the realm to investigate. Now, when the message came to Winter Plum's house, it was noon. Suddenly, there were two male pheasants that appeared on the roof, stuck out their necks, and crowed. When the messengers saw this, they were shocked. They immediately dashed into the house, knelt down, and cried repeatedly,

"Empress! Empress!"

Winter Plum's brother and sister-in-law were so scared that it was as if they had lost their souls. They told the messengers that they only had an ugly sister and that the empress was not there. Yet, the messengers insisted Winter Plum mount a horse. Her brother and sister-in-law didn't know what to say, but Winter Plum simply agreed.

Since she was so ugly and dirty, her sister-in-law had to help her clean up, combing her hair to make her presentable. Up to that time, her sister-in-law had never given her enough food and had always asked her to feed the pigs and herd the cows. Moreover, she had never given her jewelry. Despite all this, she was her sister-in-law, and now Winter Plum was to marry an emperor. So, she said to Winter Plum, "What would you like to eat? It is about time to eat."

"Cook some rice porridge for me, please!"

"You are so naïve. You are about to get on the horse for the journey. Don't you think that is too watery?"

"I want porridge! I want porridge!" Winter Plum insisted.

Her sister-in-law began to cook while her stomach grumbled. As she cooked, she thought it was funny because Winter Plum was so naïve and never asked for anything. After she made a pot of porridge, Winter Plum ate it all without stopping, and she even put a mouthful of popcorn into her mouth. Then she went to the horse, and just as she was about to mount it, she spit out the popcorn kernels in her mouth, and all the kernels turned into gold beads rolling all over. When her sister-in-law saw this, she rushed to pick up the beads. While doing this, she happened to hit Winter Plum's back. Suddenly, there was a loud clanking: Winter Plum's scabs, pockmarks, and raggedy clothes all fell to the ground. Winter Plum's hair turned thick and black. Her face started to shine; her clothes were splendid; and she became an incomparably beautiful woman. With people surrounding her, she gave the horse a kick and went on her way.

36 ■ Old Wolf

There was once an old woman named Zhang Sansao (the third daughter-in-law of the Zhangs), who left her home in the village of Dongwang and asked her three daughters to look after the house. Before she departed, she bought some baked pancakes and fried pancakes and went alone to see her old mother. On her way, she felt tired, so she sat down on a stone bench along the roadside to take a rest. She also ate a little pancake since she was hungry.

When she looked around her, she suddenly saw an ugly, naked woman coming toward her from the south. Frightened she said to herself, "How ugly she is!"

As soon as the naked woman came closer to her, she wondered what she should do. Now, when the naked woman stood in front of Zhang Sansao, she asked, "Where are you going? What is in your bag?"

"I am going to see my mother. There are some baked pancakes and fried pancakes in my bag. Why aren't you wearing clothes?" Zhang Sansao asked.

"Oh, don't mention it. I am also going to see my mother who lives in the Village of Gouer. She became sick two days ago, and I also bought some baked pancakes and fried pancakes to see her. Soon after I got on the road, an evil man took all my food and robbed me of all my clothes. I was so scared!" said the naked woman.

"You must be hungry now," replied Zhang Sansao.

"Indeed. I am very hungry. Would you do me a favor and give me a pancake to eat?"

"How about a baked pancake and a fried pancake?" said Zhang Sansao, handing over the pancakes to the naked woman.

"Thank you so . . ." the naked woman swallowed the pancakes before she finished speaking. Then she said, while staring viciously at Zhang Sansao, "Your pancakes taste so delicious. Could you give me another two?"

"Here they are. But I didn't buy a lot and should keep some for my old mother," Zhang Sansao said as she handed over the pancakes.

The naked woman took the pancakes and began to eat, while asking, "Where does your mother live? Where do you live? How many people are in your family? I am very grateful for your kindness. Indeed, we shall be friends in the future."

"My mother lives in the village of Renci. I live in Dongwang. I have only three daughters in my family. They are at home watching the house, so I should return home as soon as possible today. My eldest daughter is called First Door Bolt, and the second daughter is called Second Door Bolt, and the third daughter is called Broom Stick. When you have time, please drop by. We don't have protocols in my family."

Now, this naked woman was really an old wolf, who could transform himself into a human being, but without clothes. While he was listening to Zhang Sansao, he thought, "I can have a big feast today!" So, he suddenly appeared to be very ferocious and said vehemently, "Big Sister! Why don't you let me eat all of your pancakes? I am very hungry. If you don't, I will eat you up!"

Now, there were no other people on the road or in the field except the two of them, Zhang Sansao and the naked woman—that is, the old wolf, who we'll now call Old Wolf. Zhang Sansao had never experienced this kind of situation and was very timid. Consequently, she felt she had no choice and said, "I can't give you any more. I am bringing these to my mother. Please forgive me."

Old Wolf suddenly became very brutal and said, "If you don't let me eat the pancakes, I'll eat you first! Look at who I am!"

He turned around and suddenly turned himself into a frightening wolf and stared at Zhang Sansao with two terrifying eyes. Zhang Sansao was scared to death. She wanted to shout for help, but she knew there were no other people around. Therefore, she had to give Old Wolf all of her pancakes.

Old Wolf was indeed greedy and atrocious. As soon as he finished eating all the pancakes, he wanted to eat Zhang Sansao. Then he said, "Well, Big Sister! Let me wear your clothes so I can go and see my mother. Hand them over and be quick about it!"

Zhang Sansao hesitated and said, "I am a woman. How can I take off clothes in the wilderness and give them to you? Please forgive me. I can't take them off. Really!"

Old Wolf got very angry and said, "You don't want to take off your clothes for me? Well, then I'll eat you up!"

Zhang Sansao was so scared that she quickly took off her blouse and gave it to Old Wolf, who changed into a woman. However, Old Wolf was not satisfied and said, "Take off your pants for me. . . ."

"I am a woman. How can I take off my pants and give them to you? It would be too shameful. I can't take them off," she said with great embarrassment.

"What? You won't take them off? Then I will eat you up," and he then turned into a wolf. Therefore, she bashfully took off her pants and gave them to Old Wolf. There were still no other people on the road. Old Wolf put on the blouse and pants and felt smug. When he looked at his two feet, he realized they were without socks and shoes. When he touched his head, he felt his tousled hair, and he needed a cap to cover his head. So, he made a last request, "I am sorry to say this, but you must give me your socks, shoes, and cap. Otherwise, I will eat you up!"

Zhang Sansao was already scared to death and felt she was losing her mind. She didn't know what to do except to take off her socks, shoes, and cap. Then she handed them over to Old Wolf. Now, Zhang Sansao was completely naked, trembling in the wilderness.

Old Wolf put on the socks, shoes, and cap, and asked, "Do I look like a human now?"

"Yes, indeed," Zhang Sansao replied unconsciously.

Old Wolf now felt quite content. He looked around and didn't see anyone. Therefore, he changed into the wolf form. After howling a few times, he said to Zhang Sansao, "Now I can finally eat you up and then go to your house to eat the three girls!"

And without further ado, the Old Wolf swallowed Zhang Sansao.

After eating up the woman, Old Wolf eagerly sought to eat the three girls. Therefore, he rushed to Dongwang. Once in the village, he turned himself into a woman and asked around and found out where Zhang Sansao's house was. As soon as he knew, he dashed to the house. After he arrived at the house, he saw that the door was locked tightly. That was common for the families of the village, to prevent strangers entering their houses. Old Wolf stretched his front foot shaped like a human hand and softly tapped the doorbell. Immediately, he heard a soft voice, "Who is it? Who is knocking at the door? Is Mom back?"

Old Wolf listened and was sure it was one of the sisters' voices. Therefore, he quickly replied with his normal husky voice, "Oh, yeah. It's me. Come on! Open the door. I'm tired."

The eldest sister, First Door Bolt, heard someone speaking and didn't recognize their mother's voice. The girls often heard their mother speaking crisply, but not hoarsely like this. Therefore, she decided not to open the door and said, "You're not our Mom. Her voice is not so husky. Instead, it's clear like flowing water and crisp like a big melon. She doesn't sound as hoarse as you do. You're not our Mom. You must be a vicious woman! Your voice reveals that! I won't open the door."

Old Wolf got nervous and thought to himself, "Such a tender girl should be eaten up only by me!" But then he had a second thought, "Don't I know their names? If I call them by their names, they must believe that I am their mother. Then they would open the door for me."

When he thought about this, Old Wolf felt happy. So, he quickly said with his husky voice, "First Door Bolt, Second Door Bolt, Broom Stick! Come and open the door!"

Believe it or not, that really worked!

Inside the house, the three sisters thought, "She must be Mom. Otherwise, how can she know our names? Maybe we should open the door and take a look."

Therefore, they decided to open the door. However, as soon as they opened the door, the three sisters were frightened. Old Wolf quickly entered the room, and the girls shrieked while Old Wolf replied to them:

"Mom, Mom! How come your voice is so husky?"

"The wind's changed my voice. . . ."

"Mom, Mom! How come your eyes are so swollen?"

"I've been struck by anger. . . ."

"Mom, Mom! How come your nose is so high?"

"I hit it on a rock. . . ."

"Mom, Mom! How come your hands are so big?"

"I shook them while walking. . . ."

"Mom, Mom! How come your feet are so big?"

"I fell on the road. . . ."

"Mom, Mom! Is our grandma recovered?"

"Recovered for sure. . . ."

As they asked and Old Wolf answered, it turned late. The sun began to set, and the night shadows appeared. Soon after supper, they got ready for bed, and Old Wolf said, "Let's make a change for tonight's sleep. I suggest that the four of us sleep in the same bed because I met an old ghost on my way, and I'm very scared. I am scared even now thinking about it. If I tell you, you kids will also be scared. Therefore, I think it's best if the four of us sleep together in the same bed. First Door Bolt and Second Door Bolt, you're to sleep on the other side of the bed, and I'll hold your younger sister on this side."

They all agreed and got ready to go to bed. Old Wolf was very happy now! He thought to himself, "After First Door Bolt and Second Door Bolt fall asleep, I'll eat up Broom Stick, and then eat up those two sisters. Isn't this wonderful?"

It was time for sleeping. They turned off the lamp, took off their clothes, got into the bed, covered themselves with quilts, and fell asleep. While they were sleeping, First Door Bolt kicked her legs and stretched her feet onto Old Wolf's hips. She was immediately shocked because Old Wolf's hips were so hairy. In fact, it was Old Wolf's tail.

First Door Bolt quickly asked, "Mom, Mom! What is between your hips?"

"Some hemps."

"Where did you get them?"

"From your grandma's home."

Then, First Door Bolt stopped asking questions, and everyone became quiet and went to sleep. Since Old Wolf had some plans in mind, he did not go to sleep. As First Door Bolt and Second Door Bolt fell sound asleep, Broom Stick also fell asleep. Old Wolf softly coughed twice, and heard nothing from the sisters. Then he thought, "They must be in a deep sleep now. I'll begin by first eating up the third sister."

Then, he took a bite and killed the third sister. At first, he began to eat slowly. He ate the head, and then two arms, two hands, the heart, the intestines like noodle soup, and then two legs. As he was about to eat the two feet, First Door Bolt and Second Door Bolt suddenly woke up and heard Old Wolf gobbling and crunching. They wondered what the noise was and could not help but ask:

"Mom, Mom! What are you eating?"

"Salty dry turnips."

"Where did you buy them?"

"They are taken from your grandma's home."

"Give us some."

"No. Kids should not eat this. I eat it to cure coughing. Didn't you hear my voice getting husky?"

"Mom! Give us some. We've never eaten that."

"No. Kids should not eat this."

"Mom! Give us some."

"You annoying girls. You're helpless. Now take a bite!"

Then, Old Wolf threw a little toe at First Door Bolt, who cried: "Oh, no! Isn't this the toe of our little sister? Was our little sister eaten up by a wolf? Second Sister! This is not our Mom. This old woman must be Old Wolf! Let's run quickly!"

The two sisters talked to each other in secret and made a plan to escape. First Door Bolt and Second Door Bolt decided to escape by saying that they had to go caca outside. Once outside, they would climb up a tree and call for help. Therefore, according to their plan, First Door Bolt shouted, "Mom, Mom! I want to go caca."

"Do it next to the bed."

"No, no. The holy God of Bed is there."

"Do it behind the door."

"No, no. The holy God of Door is there."

"Do it behind the stove."

"No, no. The holy God of Stove is there."

"Do it outside!"

First Door Bolt quickly ran outside. There was a tall elm tree next to the house, and she quickly climbed up the tree.

Then Second Door Bolt shouted, "Mom, Mom! I want to poop."

"Do it next to the bed."

"No, no. The holy God of Bed is there."

"Do it behind the door."

"No, no. The holy God of Door is there."

"Do it behind the stove."

"No, no. The holy God of Stove is there."

"Do it outside!"

Second Door Bolt quickly ran outside and also climbed up the tree, where the two sisters were now both sad and cheerful. They were sad because their Mom and younger sister had been eaten up by Old Wolf. Yet, they were cheerful because they had escaped.

Old Wolf waited and waited, but First Door Bolt and Second Door Bolt did not return, He got nervous, and shouted in bed, "First Door Bolt! Second Door Bolt! Where are you two damn girls? Come back! Haven't you finished pooping?"

First Door Bolt and Second Door Bolt heard Old Wolf shouting and shouted back, "Crystal colorful octagon well! Crystal colorful heptagon stars! Mom, Mom! Come on out to see this beautiful scene!"

Old Wolf came out and saw the two sisters up in the tree. Immediately, he became very angry and shouted, "You damn girls! Why are you up in the tree? Come on down!"

First Door Bolt and Second Door Bolt sang together, "Crystal colorful octagon well! Crystal colorful heptagon stars! Mom, Mom! Come on out to see this beautiful scene!"

Old Wolf was upset and said, "You damn girls! How can I get up there?"

The two sisters said, "Mom, Mom! There is big rope behind the door. Go and get it, and tie one end to your waist, and throw the other end to us, so we can pull you up."

Old Wolf heard and thought it was the right idea. He found the rope and tied one end to his waist, and threw the other end to the sisters. He wanted to be pulled up so that he could devour the sisters. Meanwhile, the two sisters pulled and pulled hard. Eventually, they caused the Old Wolf's stomach to hurt very much. Then, when they pulled the Old Wolf halfway up in the air, they let go of the rope, with the result that Old Wolf fell head first. . . .

"You damn girls! Why did you drop me?" Old Wolf shouted.

"Mom, Mom! Our hands were too loose and that's why you fell upside down. Mom, Mom! Let's try it again!"

The two sisters pulled and pulled hard, and again caused Old Wolf's stomach to hurt very much. When they pulled Old Wolf halfway up into the air, they let go of the rope and Old Wolf again fell down. They did this seven or eight times, and Old Wolf's stomach broke, and all the hairs on his hips was rubbed off. Old Wolf was extremely furious, and took the rope off his waist and said, "I'll go inside to sharpen my teeth, and then I'll come back to devour you two sisters!"

When Old Wolf returned to the house, he felt very weary and wanted to smoke a pipe to get some energy. He walked into the dark room to search for the pipe and tobacco plate. Owing to the darkness, he touched a large scorpion, which bit a big hole in his paw. Old Wolf could not find any fire to light the pipe, so he went to the stove in the kitchen. Old Wolf stirred the ashes and touched a Duck Egg spirit, which exploded. The explosion blinded Old Wolf, and he cried, "Bad luck! Bad luck!" as he ran out. Once outside, he ran into the Cow Dung spirit, which twisted and threw Old Wolf on the ground. Then the Stick spirit came from the south. After learning what had happened, the Stick spirit began to beat Old Wolf with sticks, one blow after another, until Old Wolf died.

民間敵話之一

怪兄弟

林蘭 編

上海

北新書局印行

1932

Once there was a middle-aged woman who was returning to her home. She carried a basket with some sugar cake and delicious dumplings in it. On her way, she met Old Wolf's Wife.

"Where are you going?" Old Wolf's Wife asked.

"I am returning to my home."

"What are you carrying?"

"Some sugar cake and delicious dumplings."

"Give me some to eat!"

"No. I can't give you any!"

Old Wolf's Wife then had an idea, and she said, "Look, there is a bug crawling on your head!"

"Catch it and show me!"

That was exactly what Old Wolf's Wife expected. Therefore, the woman sat down on the roadside. While Old Wolf's Wife searched and caught the bug on her head, she learned that the woman had three daughters at home. The eldest was called Onion, the second daughter was called Plate, and the third was called Pan. Old Wolf's Wife used her fingernails to cut up the woman and ate her up, and then she ate all the things in the basket.

Then, Old Wolf's Wife put on the woman's clothes, went to the woman's home, and knocked on the door, "Onion, Plate, and Pan, come and open the door for Mom."

The eldest daughter ran to the door, took a peek, and said, "You're not my Mom. My Mom's feet are small, but yours are big."

"I pushed the grindstone at grandma's home and made my feet big."

But the eldest daughter did not open the door.

The second daughter ran to the door, took a peek, and said, "You're not my Mom. My Mom doesn't have pockmarks on her face, but you have."

"I slept on the beans in your grandma's home, and that's how I got these pockmarks."

However, the second daughter did not open the door.

The third daughter, Pan, said to her sisters, "Why don't you open the door for Mom?"

Unlike her sisters, she ran to the door and opened it.

Now Old Wolf's Wife entered the room. The eldest daughter dragged a bench over to her, but she did not sit. The second daughter moved over a chair to her, but she did not sit. The third daughter brought over a measuring dipper, and Old Wolf's Wife sat in it with her tail hiding inside the dipper, making some noises.

"What are those noises?" the daughters asked.

"Oh, I caught a mouse from your grandma's home."

By the evening, Old Wolf's Wife asked the daughters to sleep with her in the same bed. The eldest and the second daughter were not willing, but the third daughter listened and slept with her. By midnight, the eldest and the second daughter could not sleep, but heard a loud gobbling sound. They asked, "What are you eating?"

"The carrots I brought back from your grandma's home."

"Give us some to eat."

"No, you shouldn't eat, or you will get a stomachache."

After a little while, they heard the glugging sound of drinking.

"What are you drinking?"

"Some rice wine I brought back from your grandma's home."

"Give us some to drink."

"No, you shouldn't drink, or you'll get headache."

The two daughters realized something bad had happened, and wanted to escape. But they didn't dare try. Instead, they pretended they wanted to poop.

"We want to poop."

"The pot is under our bed."

"It smells bad."

"Go to the corner of the room."

"It still smells bad."

"Go outside."

So, the two daughters ran outside. By then, it was already morning, and they ran to the backyard, where they climbed up a big tree above the dunghill, and shouted,

"East neighbors and west neighbors!

Come and see.

Old Wolf's Wife came to our house,

Ate our littler sister,

And wanted to eat us, too."

Old Wolf's Wife saw that the two sisters had not returned to the room. Therefore, she ran out, and when she saw them on the tree, she shouted at them, "Why are you up there?"

"Oh, Mom! Come and see! There is a wedding next door."

"Really? Let me get up there! Let me get up there!"

She wanted to climb the tree, but did not succeed. The two sisters came down and used a rope to pull her up. Just as she was up close to the branch, they let go of the rope and said, "Oh, no. Mom is choking to death!"

"It doesn't matter. Just quickly pull me up," Old Wolf's Wife cried.

So, they pulled her up again. Just as she was up close to the branch, they suddenly let go of the rope again, causing the Old Wolf's Wife to choke to death. Then, they buried her in the dunghill.

38 ■ Brother Moon and Sister Sun

Nowadays, the sun comes out at daytime, and the moon comes out at nighttime. The sunlight is bright with a dazzling glare, and the moonlight is like silver and water. However, these are the results of the following story.

The sun and the moon were brother and sister. The sun was the elder brother, and the moon was the younger sister. They were very close to each other, and their job was to shed light upon the human world. Originally, the moon appeared in daytime and the sun at nighttime. However, a long time ago, the two of them met and had a heartfelt conversation. The sun exclaimed that everything at night was good except for one thing—he didn't feel content because many people would take a bath during the night. It was embarrassing if a girl took a bath.

"Well," said the moon, "Let's switch."

Then, they switched their roles, but the moon was not completely at ease, so she used her embroidering needle to stab those who would look at her.

民間故事之一

In ancient times, there was a man who went fishing every day. He would catch fish with a square net along a river in order to support his family of three consisting of his mother, his wife, and himself. Surprisingly, he did not catch any fish for two days. On the third day, he still did not catch any fish. By the evening, it began to rain. Usually, the fish he caught for the whole day would sell for very little money, amounting to one day's food. Now, three days without any money, how could he not be annoyed? Just as he was becoming very upset, he suddenly felt something in the net. So, he pulled it a little bit and thought there was a big fish. Quickly, he pulled up the net and saw something rolling in the net in the dark. He tried to be brave and shouted, "It is a ghost! It is a ghost! Wife! Wife! Get me a rope, quickly! I will tie it up! This thing has prevented me from catching any fish!"

His wife heard there was a ghost and became very scared. She quickly found a rope that was for tying crabs and brought it to her husband. As he was about to tie up the thing, it shouted, "Don't tie me up! Don't tie me up! I'll help you catch fish!"

"Aren't you a ghost?" asked the man. "How can you help me?"

"Yes, yes. I am a drowned ghost," said the dark thing. "I can push fish about in the water, and I can drive them to your net."

"Then I will not tie you up," said the man.

He then put down his square net into the water. After a while, he pulled it up, and there were many big fish jumping all about. One day passed. Another day passed. The man and the ghost got along very well. Therefore, soon they became brothers and followed a traditional custom: they called each other elder brother and younger brother, and the water ghost became elder brother.

The man often bought some wine and dishes and brought them to the riverbank to drink and eat with the water ghost. Three years passed by quickly. One night, there was bright moonlight on the riverbank. The water ghost rolled out of the water and said to the fisherman, "My younger brother! My good brother! I have to leave now."

"Elder brother! How come you are leaving?"

"I have been here for three years now. The time is up. I have to seek a new life elsewhere. Tomorrow, two women will arrive to fetch water from the river. They are sisters-in-law. I have to choose one body and reside in it. When you see them, please don't make any noise."

Indeed, two women came to fetch water from the river. Because the daughter-in-law was wronged by her mother-in-law, she wanted to jump into the river as she got to the waterfront. The fisherman dashed over, grabbed her tightly, and called the younger girl to help him pull up her sister-in-law.

That evening, the water ghost rolled out of the water to the bank, and stomped his feet. In addition, he shouted: "My younger brother! You hurt me so much! Missing this opportunity means I have to wait for another three years!"

"Elder brother! Elder brother! They were two lives! If the daughter-in-law threw herself into the river, her sister-in-law would panic and would certainly jump in, right?"

"I forgive you. You have such a kind heart," said the water ghost. He continued driving fish to the net every day.

Another three years passed by quickly. The two of them got along so well that others all said they were closer than blood brothers. One night, the water ghost said to the fisherman, "My younger brother! My younger brother! I have to leave now."

"Elder brother, are you going to find a body to seek a new life?" asked the fisherman.

"No. Not so. The King of Hell is sending me to a city to become the city god."

"Elder brother, I really don't want you to leave. I'll miss you so much."

"But we have no choice even if you miss me so much," said the water ghost. They both wept. Finally, the water ghost said, "In case you are ever in trouble, you can find me in a certain place."

After the water ghost left, the fisherman could no longer catch as much fish. Then, there were two days when he caught nothing. On the third day, he caught a big red fish ten feet long. Since there was a rich man who wanted to eat a big fish, he sent his chef to buy the fish with fifty ounces of silver. The two chefs prepared the fish and put it in a pot. All at once, there was a delicious smell, and they felt like tasting the fish.

"Since the fish is so big," the two said to each other, "we can surely eat some, and it wouldn't be noticed."

But they kept eating one bite after another and could not stop until they ate all the meat on the fish's back. Then they felt their bodies became so light that they raised their hands and flew up to the sky.

Now it was lunchtime, and the rich man was waiting to eat the big fish. However, he waited and waited and still did not see the fish. Soon, he became so annoyed that he sent his servant to the kitchen to check. The servant saw no one there, but smelled the delicious fish from the pot and began drooling.

"Since the fish has already been eaten up like this," he said to himself, "I can just eat a little, and no one will find out."

However, he was as greedy as the chefs were, and one bite led to another until he ate up all the fish meat. Then, he felt his body was so light that he raised his hands and flew up to the sky.

The master was still waiting, but his servant did not return. He got so angry that he himself ran to the kitchen, shouting curses all along the way. When he arrived in the kitchen, he didn't find a single person, but there was some leftover fish soup in the pot. He was outraged, stomped his feet, and cursed loudly. Suddenly, he heard a voice from above, "Master! Quickly, drink the fish soup!"

He raised his head and saw the two chefs and the servant standing in white clouds. The master now knew that they had eaten the fish and had become immortals. So, he quickly drank the fish soup from the pot. He raised his hands, and wanted to fly up to the sky, but he couldn't. He was simply not fated to become an immortal!

Now, let's not talk any more about the master, but look at the fisherman. After he caught the big red fish, he could no longer catch any fish. He now had only the fifty ounces of silver to support his mother and wife. The whole family had to rely upon him for clothes and food. How could they survive like this? In less than half a year, they became so poor that they did not have enough food to eat. Therefore, he then thought about seeking out his elder brother for help and went to the designated place and found the city temple. His ghost brother was not home, but his ghost wife was home. The fisherman bought some incense and joss paper, and burned them in front of the seat of his ghost elder brother, while saying some prayers to him. Then, he went out on the street to take a walk.

In the evening, when his ghost brother returned, he saw some ashes in front of his seat and asked his wife, "Who burned this?"

"I don't know who he is. I only heard him calling you elder brother when he was burning the paper," the woman said.

"That must be my younger brother!" said the ghost brother. Then, he immediately sent his little ghost followers to find the fisherman and bring him back.

"Elder brother! Elder brother! I am poor now. Please help me!" said the fisherman.

"You'd better go home right now. Your wife is dying," the ghost brother warned him.

"Can't you save her?"

"I don't have the book of life and death in hand. How can I save her?"

The fisherman begged him repeatedly. The ghost brother pulled out ten strings of money and said, "Take this money as your fare. When you get home, don't tell your wife why, but just fill the room with grass. Paste paper everywhere in the room to diminish the light. Then buy three pounds of wheat, and make flour paste together with your wife. Ask her to make pancakes for three days and three nights. Then she will not die."

The fisherman took the ten strings of money and hurried away. When he got home, he didn't say a word but filled the room with dry grass, tore down the old paper couplets, and pasted all the bright places with paper. His wife asked him to eat, but he refused. He ran to the street and bought some wheat with the leftover money. He then called his wife to make flour paste after hulling the wheat and then asked her to make pancakes without sleeping. His wife was confused by the way he did all these things. As she was making pancakes, she said, "You want me make so many pancakes. How can we finish eating them?"

"Don't talk. Just make pancakes!" said the fisherman.

She had no choice but to make the pancakes. The fisherman took care of the fire in the stove, and his wife tended to the pancakes. His mother was sitting next to the stove, and when she became hungry, she just grabbed some pancakes and ate. Two days and two nights passed. Now, the fisherman and his mother fell asleep. The fisherman's wife was still awake, but her eyes were blood-red. She became angry, but she didn't lose her temper. She was busy making pancakes and taking care of the fire.

By the third day, the grass was almost used up. She pushed her husband, and asked him to get some grass from outside. But she could not wake him up. His mother was also in a sound sleep. She had to put some grass in the stove, and took the basket to get grass outside. As she opened the door, she saw many small ghosts standing in the yard, holding ropes, and throwing them at her. She was frightened and fell on the ground with a loud cry. Now, the fisherman suddenly woke from his dream. He saw his wife dead right in front of the door. He hammered his chest and cursed himself, "You are such a sleeping dead pig. Why did you want to sleep at this time?"

Some days passed. He became even poorer. Now, he wanted to find his ghost brother again. He went to the city temple. With tears, he told his ghost brother what had happened, "Elder brother! My wife is dead."

"Why did you fall asleep? Now she is the wife of the ghost messenger in the south temple," the ghost brother said.

"I miss her! Can you take me there to see her?"

"She would ignore you even if you go to see her," said the ghost brother.

He insisted on seeing her, and the elder brother had to take him there. He saw his wife sitting in a small room doing some sewing. He called her, but she didn't answer.

"Go home," said the ghost brother. "Go home! Your fortune has run out."

When they returned to the city temple, the fisherman said, "Elder brother! Can I do something for you?"

"No. You can't. Only ghosts can do things for me."

"Well, I have nothing to do here. Won't I starve to death?"

"It is almost the time for the west temple to hold a show. I can recommend that you join the troupe and play the drums," the ghost brother said.

"Good. I can make a living by playing the drums," said the fisherman.

The ghost brother went to the west temple that night and sent a dream to the leader of the troupe, "Tomorrow, a person will come and want the job of playing the drums. Don't reject him."

At daybreak, the fisherman went to the leader of the troupe and said, "I would like to play the drums in your troupe. Will you accept me?"

The leader recalled the dream in which he heard what the city god told him. How could he not accept? The fisherman then played the drums. When there was singing on the stage, he played the drums, but he also played the drums when there was no singing. He didn't know when to play and when not to play, but just kept playing. In less than two days, he broke the drums with four or five big holes.

The fisherman dropped the mallets, ran to the city temple, and said to the ghost brother, "I can't play the drums. Are there other things that I can do?"

"Of course, yes. There is a big mountain in the northwest, about one hundred miles away. There are a lot of hairy people on the mountain. They have eaten many local people. They never come out of their cave during the day. You are to go and build a mortar wall to block the cave. Then pour tung oil on it. The old hairy man is short-tempered. When he can't come out of the cave, he will hit the wall with his head and kill himself. He will be wearing a cap and a red shirt. Those are treasures. You are to take the cap and put it on your head. Then take the shirt and wear it so that others cannot see you. Here, I have a sword. Take it with you, and use it to kill the little hairy people. If you get rid of those monsters for the local people, they will surely give you a lot of gold and silver."

The fisherman took the sword, and set off to the northwest. The sun was about to set when he arrived at the place of the hairy people. He saw many houses, big and small, but all were closed, and he heard men and women crying. When he arrived at an inn, it was already closed. He begged the owner for a room, and finally he was allowed to come in through the door, which was slightly opened for him. As soon as he sat down inside and closed the door, he heard heavy footsteps from outside, along with some shouting noises, as if a fist were pounding on the door and walls. He knew it was the time that the hairy people went down the mountain. By the time the rooster crowed, the noise from outside faded away.

The fisherman waited until daybreak and then took the sword and bought some tung oil to carry into the mountain. He found the cave, built a mortar wall at the entrance, and poured the tung oil on it. When the sun set, the old hairy man came to the entrance, wearing a cap on his head and a small red shirt, humming a local tune. A few hundred small hairy people were following him. When he saw the wall, he shouted, "What's blocking my way? Tear it down quickly! Otherwise, I must eat you up!"

The fisherman hid behind the wall and kept quiet. The old hairy man began to climb the wall, but the wall was covered with tung oil, and he kept sliding down as he tried to climb up. He lost his temper and suddenly hit the wall with his head. Then, his head broke into eighteen pieces, and he dropped down dead. His cap and shirt also fell on the ground, and the small hairy people were all so scared that they ran back into the cave, crying like ghosts.

Now, the fisherman quickly tore down the wall, raised his sword, and entered the cave. He picked up the cap and the red shirt and put them on. He then dashed into the cave and killed the small hairy people one by one. As their heads fell to the ground, they couldn't tell who had killed them. Soon, he killed them all. He came out of the cave and put away the cap and the red shirt. He dragged the body of the old hairy man and walked toward the village. Quickly word spread, and all the villagers knew that he had killed the old hairy man and all the small hairy people. Everyone was so joyful that they danced and danced. Then, they rushed to give him gold and silver.

However, I've been told that he was wearing the hairy man's cap and red shirt, and the people could not see him. He then did many bad things. This is all I've heard. What happened next? I don't know. You'll have to find other people to tell you.

40 ■ The One-Legged Child

Once there was a boy named Little Bald who was very poor and lived with his mother without a father or brothers. He was hired by his maternal uncle to herd the cows and gather grass. One day, he was supposed to gather grass, but he wanted to take the day off just to play.

"If you don't go gathering grass, what will the cattle eat?" his uncle asked.

"What if I pull out some beans from the field instead? Would that be all right?" he replied.

"No! Go and gather the grass!" shouted his uncle.

Therefore, Little Bald went to cut the grass. Then, he came to a spot where the grass kept growing as he cut. The more he cut the grass, the taller it grew. It was endless. So, he went to the same spot every day to cut grass.

One day, an elephant came, and it took the boy to a big valley and gave him a basketful of ivory that he dragged home.

"Oh, my! How precious the ivory is!" his mother exclaimed. "I can't wait to sell it at the market."

The boy continued to go to the same spot to cut grass. One day, there came a group of beasts that surrounded a one-legged child. Little Bald was so scared of them that he rolled into the hole of a tree trunk in a hurry. Suddenly, there was a storm with thunder, and the beasts ran to the mountains, leaving the one-legged child alone. Little Bald thought, "It would be good if the storm passes quickly."

Soon, his wish was fulfilled, and the thunder and rain ended. Then, he jumped out of the hole of the tree trunk, raised his sickle, and cut off the single leg of the child. The child suddenly disappeared with a loud cry.

Later, Little Bald went and sold the ivory at the market. At the end of the day, he had a bag of money that he had to carry on his shoulders. This made it difficult to walk home, as it was getting dark. Now the one-legged child turned into a woman, crying at the roadside. Little Bald asked, "Auntie, Auntie, why are you crying?"

"I don't have a father, I don't have a mother, and I don't have a husband. How miserable it is to be alone without any relatives. How could I not cry?" she said.

"How would you like to be my wife? I have a full bag of money," he said.

The woman wiped her tears and said, "How wonderful!"

Little Bald took her home, and his mother was so happy when she learned that he had brought home a wife. Next morning, Little Bald went to the market to sell ivory again, and once again, he ended the day with a bag of money that was difficult to carry home since it was getting dark. An old man came toward him and asked, "Would you like to be my god-son? Let me save your life!"

"What disaster is awaiting me?" Little Bald asked.

"I can tell fortunes. Didn't you take a wife to your home yesterday? That woman was once the one-legged child, and she intends to kill you!"

"Oh, I want to be your god-son," said Little Bald anxiously. "Please save me!"

"All right," said the old man. "Take this piece of spell, and when you get home, paste it on her head. Then you will be safe."

Little Bald arrived home and pasted the spell on the woman's head. All at once, the woman changed back to her original form and fell dead to the ground.

41 ■ The Fairy Cave

A long time ago, there were two brothers, one named Liu Chen, and the other Ruan Zhao. They were maternal first cousins. One day, they went to fetch water in a valley. It was March, and the mountains were covered with green grass and beautiful colorful flowers. The young men put aside the water buckets to take a good look at the scene. They climbed from one hilltop to another and went farther and farther, until they reached the end of the path. Once there, they saw a cave among the rocks that had a large entrance. Inside, two fairies were sitting and playing chess. The two brothers quietly sneaked to the entrance of the cave and watched the two women. There was a white rabbit at the feet of the fairies, and it jumped back and forth. When it jumped to one side, the grass turned green. When it jumped to the other side, the grass turned yellow. The flowers at the entrance also opened and closed as the rabbit jumped. The two brothers found this very strange.

As the two fairies now finished their game of chess, they raised their heads and saw the two brothers. "When did you get here?" they asked.

"Quite a while ago," they quickly replied, wanting to depart.

"You can stay here in the cave. You don't have to return home. Actually, even if you return home, no one would recognize you any longer."

The two brothers did not understand the fairies and said, "No, no, no. We must return home."

The fairies knew that they couldn't keep the two brothers in the cave, so they took out two sticks and said, "If you don't feel content outside the cave, you can come inside. Use the stick to touch the cave door, and it will open."

The two brothers each took a stick and left. They came to the valley and found the place where they had set down the water buckets and shoulder poles. However, they saw that the buckets had now turned into a pile of mud. Before this, there hadn't been any trees around the valley, but now there was a very tall pine tree. All of this fascinated the brothers. When they returned to their village, they couldn't find the gates to their two houses. However, they saw two white-haired men sitting next to a pile of hay. Therefore, they went up and asked, "Where are the gates to Liu Chen and Ruan Zhao's houses?"

"Liu Chen and Raun Zhao are our ancestors. We are their seventh-generation descendants. How can you young people mention our ancestors' names without respect?"

Now, you must indeed feel strange as you listen to this tale. How can the young men Liu Chen and Ruan Zhao have seventh-generation grandchildren? Well, it turned out that when the white rabbit in the Fairy Cave jumped back and forth one round, it was one year for the human world. They stayed in the cave half a day, but it was already four or five hundred years in the human world.

Liu Chen and Ruan Zhao became very confused when they heard the two old men's words. They stared at the two old men and said, "We are Liu Chen and Ruan Zhao!"

The two old men became furious, and their beards started shaking. They called all the villagers to curse them and to beat them up. "You damn demons! How dare you take advantage of us old people?"

Liu Chen and Ruan Zhao became frightened and ran away. They did not stop until they arrived at the entrance to the Fairy Cave, where they saw that the door was tightly closed. Now, they remembered that they had lost the sticks in their hands. They wanted to go back to the village to find them, but were afraid that they would be beaten. Therefore, they tapped on the door and shouted. However, there was no answer. They were so fearful and anxious that they hit their heads on the door and died.

The celestial emperor felt pity for them when they died. Therefore, he named Liu Chen as the God of Increasing Fortune, and Ruan Zhao, the God of Snatching Fortune.

42 ■ Increasing Fortune and Snatching Fortune

One day, the God of Increasing Fortune and the God of Snatching Fortune were riding their Fortune Clouds back home from a Long Life Peach Feast. On their way, they took a walk on a promenade up in the sky, just to digest the food in their stomachs. As if boasting, the God of Increasing Fortune said: "Elder Brother Snatching Fortune, you are such a trickster and are just like a little monkey. Now, lower your head and look at the people on the ground, carefully! They are crying owing to cold and hunger, helpless with illnesses, and do not even have tombs for themselves after death. How pitiful these people are! I have never been able to bear seeing people suffering, and I always give them something to survive and to make their lives more pleasurable. However, you, my elder brother, a trickster monkey, you just like making fun of these people. You don't even allow them to enjoy the little things that I give them. Do you enjoy being a trickster, a monkey?"

The God of Snatching Fortune merely replied with a cold smile: "Well, enough of this talk, my elder brother! We both work for the Celestial Grandfather. The difference is that you are welcomed, but I am the target of their complaints. In fact, it is a matter of fate. I never snatch people's happiness if they are fated to be happy."

"Well. You are quibbling! Every time I bless people with some money, you always find ways to snatch it back!"

"That is their fate. If you bless those children who do not deserve the money, it does not do any good for them. Even if you say it is only some material favor, and . . ."

"Nonsense!" The God of Increasing Fortune felt a little upset. "I don't believe that anyway."

"You don't believe it? Well, let's have a test. Look, there are a few people pushing wheelbarrows with their upper bodies naked, and they are sweating. Aren't they pitiful? Please bless them with a treasure, and let's see what that person does with it. I am afraid . . ."

"All right! If you don't snatch the treasures, I will bless them with dozens," the God of Increasing Fortune said. He then ordered his assistant to put dozens of shining coins along the narrow path that the people used to make their way. Then, they sat calmly in the clouds and watched how those people would react.

When the first wheelbarrow approached the money, the man stopped and proposed to his fellows, "Brother Li! Brother Wang! . . . I am not bragging. I can close my eyes and push the wheelbarrow for fifty steps!"

The others all responded, "That is nothing unusual! Every one of us can do that!"

"Well, let's all try!"

"Good, good!"

Along with the screaking noises, all the wheelbarrows passed by the shining coins. The money was still shining on the road.

"Did you see that, Brother Increasing Fortune?" the God of Snatching Fortune asked.

The God of Increasing Fortune said nothing, as if thinking of something. After a long silence, he said, "Let's continue our strolling. . . ."

The Lin Lan Series, published by North New Books (Beixin shuju, Shanghai) between 1929 and 1932, was categorized into three subgenres as *minjian chuanshuo* (folk legends and tales), *minjian tonghua* (folk fairy tales), and *minjian qushi* (comic folk tales) in 43 volumes (see also the introduction). In the folk fairy tales subgenre, there are 8 volumes with a total of 154 tales. Of the 42 tales in this translated collection, 38 tales are selected from this subgenre, and 4 tales (15, 16, 17, and 18 in part 2) are selected from the volume of *The King of Ashes* in the folk legends and tales subgenre.

Title of Volume	Volume Abbreviation	Number of Tales in Volume	Number of Volume Pages	Year of First Edition
The Fisherman's Lover (Yufu de qingren, 渔夫的情人)	FL	17	118	1929
The Golden Frog (Jin tian ji, 金田鸡)	GF	16	118	1929
The Melon King (Gua wang, 瓜王)	MK	17	116	1930
The Ghost Brother (Gui ge ge, 鬼哥哥)	GB	22	114	1930
The Garden Snake (Cai hua lang, 菜花郎)	GS	16	131	1930

Title of Volume	Volume Abbreviation	Number of Tales in Volume	Number of Volume Pages	Year of First Edition
After Replacing the Heart (Huan xin hou, 换心后)	RH	20	120	1930
The Weird Brothers (Guai xiong di, 怪兄弟)	WB	20	125	1930
The One-Footed Child (Du jiao hai zi, 独脚孩子)	OC	26	115	1932
The King of Ashes (Hui da wang, 灰大王)	KA	25	113	1932

The following bibliographical notes are given in this format: (1) order in this collection correlating to the table of contents; (2) tale title; (3) publication sources; (4) information about the contributor where available (as in the original publication); (5) tale type in the ATU system (Uther 2004); (6) tale type in the ATT system (Ting 1978).

In studying Chinese tale types, there are some other references or systems. For example, Eberhard published his German version of *Typen chinesischer Volksmärchen* (1937b), which was translated into Chinese (Ai 1999). The only English publication is Nai-tung Ting's *A Type Index of Chinese Folktales* (1978), which is translated into Chinese (Ding 1983, 2008) and is mentioned here as the ATT system.

Other important studies of Chinese tale types are in Chinese only; thus, they are not included in this tale-type note. However, they are essential for those who study Chinese tales—for example, Jin (2000–2002, 2003, 2007) published several comprehensive studies on Chinese tale types based on both the AT and ATT systems by including those excluded in the previous systems. Qi (2007) has created a system to categorize ancient Chinese folk tales. A comprehensive study on the history and contents of different systems about Chinese tale types has been completed by Chen Lina (2010).

All illustrations are from the Lin Lan Series, in the collection of Beijing Normal University Library.

	Tale Title	Chinese Title; Volume Abbreviation: Pages	Information about the Contributor	Tale Type in ATU System	Tale Type in ATT System
Part One. Love with a Fairy					
1	The Dragon Daughter	Longnü (龙女); FL: 77–82	N/A	555* 923B	555 592A
2	The Golden Pin	Duijinchai (对金钗); RH: 83–91	N/A	881A* 555	301
3	The Fisherman's Lover	Yüfu de qingren (渔夫的情人); FL: 1–12	N/A	400	400B
4	The Silkworm	Can de gushi (蚕的故事); FL: 65–68	Yi Wo [July 21, morning, Kaifeng, Henan Province]	400 440	400
5	On the Celestial Riverbank	Tianhean (天河岸); RH: 53–57	N/A	400	400D
6	The Flute Player	Chuixiaoren (吹箫人); WB: 63–67	N/A	555 592A	
7	The Pheasant Feather Cloak	Jimaoyi (鸡毛衣); WB: 68–72	N/A	465A 592A	
8	The Sea Dragon King	Hailong dawang (海龙大王); GS: 14–17	N/A	301	301 555
9	The Celestial Fairy	Huagu (华姑); GB: 46–56	Sun Qingsu	301 313A 750	301
10	The Daughter of the Dragon King of the Sea	Hailongwang de nüer (海龙王的女儿); WB: 36–58	N/A	301 555	301 555

Part Two. Predestined Love

11	The Paper Bride	Zhinüren (纸女人); OC: 97–100	Sun Jiaxun [This tale is popular in Guanyun area in Jiangsu Province.]	930A	400B
12	The Human-Bear's Death for Love	Renxiong de qingsi (人熊的情死); FL: 13–18	N/A	400 554	400E
13	The Snake Spirit	Shelangjing (蛇郎精); FL: 55–64	N/A	433	433E
14	The Garden Snake	Caiguashe de gushi (菜瓜蛇的故事); FL: 45–54	Xue Lin [with letters to the editor][1]	411 433	
15	Spouses from Two Worlds	Liangshi fuqi (两世夫妻); KA: 31–35	N/A	400 930A	
16	The Peasant's Wife	Nongfu zhiqi (农夫之妻); KA: 42–46	N/A	930A	
17	The Marriage of a Human and a Ghost	Rengui jiehun (人鬼结婚); KA: 64–67	N/A	930A	
18	The Ghost Marriage	Guihun (鬼婚); KA: 70–72	N/A	930A	
19	Golden Frog	Jintianji (金田鸡); GF: 59–64	N/A	400	
20	The Toad Son	Hamar (蛤蟆儿); FL: 33–40	N/A	440A	
21	The Chicken Egg	Jidan (鸡蛋); FL: 33–40	N/A	440A 700	
22	No Giving Up before Seeing the Yellow River	Bujian huanghe busixin (不见黄河不死心); MK: 50–58	N/A	780	780D
23	The Reward of the Snake	She de baoen (蛇的报恩); GF: 1–10	Tian Shaoqian	554D 400 747 554D	
24	Everyone Is Content	Renren ruyi (人人如意); FL: 111–115	N/A	461 465	461A

Part Three. The Hatred and Love of Siblings

25	*The Two Brothers*	*Liangxiongdi* 两兄弟(一); *FL:* 83–91	N/A	613 503	613A 503E
26	*The Yellow Bag*	*Huangkoudai* (黄口袋); *RH:* 68–77	N/A	555	555C
27	*The Two Sisters*	*Liangjiemei* (两姐妹); *WB:* 19–22	N/A	613A	
28	*The Elder Daughter*	*Danüer* (大女儿); *RH:* 94–97	N/A	503	
29	*The Three Brothers*	*Sanxiongdi fenjia* (三兄弟分家); *GF:* 75–82	Xi Sheng	503	503E
30	*Elder Brother and Younger Brother*	*Xiongdi liangge* (兄弟两个); *GF:* 83–96	N/A	503	
31	*The Melon King*	*Guawang* (瓜王); *MK:* 34–37	N/A	503 513	

Part Four. Other Odd Tales

32	*The Weird Brothers*	*Guaixiongdi* (怪兄弟); *WB:* 1–6	N/A	513	513A
33	*After Replacing the Heart*	*Huanxinhou* (换心后); *RH:* 58–62	N/A	513 700	
34	*The Hairy Girl on the Pine Tree*	*Qingsong shangde maonü* (青松上的毛女); *RH:* 78–82	N/A	510A	
35	*The Shedding Winter Plum*	*Malamei tuojia* (马腊梅脱甲); *MK:* 10–13	N/A	433	
36	*Old Wolf*	*Laolang de guishi* (老狼的故事); *RH:* 98–108	Gu Fengtian	333C	
37	*Old Wolf's Wife*	*Laolangpo* (老狼婆); *FL:* 19–25	Zhang Yuan	333C	
38	*Brother Moon and Sister Sun*	*Yueliang gege he taiyang meimei* (月亮哥哥和太阳妹妹); *GF:* 97	Recording in Wuchang, Hubei Province, October 30, 1926, by Zhou Jian	368	

(continued)

39	The Ghost Brother	Guigege (鬼哥哥); GB: 1–17	Sun Jiaxun [with postscript][2]	776 745A 465A	
40	The One-Legged Child	Dutui haizi (独腿孩子); OC: 1–3	Sun Jiaxun	700	
41	The Fairy Cave	Xiangutong (仙姑洞); GB: 31–34	Sun Jiaxun [with postscript][3]	555 313A 613A 750 922	555C
42	Increasing Fortune and Snatching Fortune	Zengfu yu lüefu (增福与掠福); GB: 35–37	Yun Cheng	745A	

Notes

1. Following the text of "The Garden Snake," there is correspondence between the contributor and the editor.

Letter from the contributor to the editor:

Dear Mr. Qiming;

Earlier I read from the *Yusi* magazine the tales about the cuckoo bird and the "*kuwa*" bird, and now just read your article. You talked about the bird in the tale of "Snake Man" and that there were humans transforming into birds. I couldn't help but recall the tales I heard from my mother when I was a boy in my hometown about several types of birds and the garden snake. I then asked my mother to tell them again. I recorded this tale as she told, in her tone.

The so-called "dong-dong-du" and "ge-zuo-ge-gong" birds are from my hometown, but they may also exist elsewhere. Birds sing alike anywhere in the world, but human beings from different places have different sounds to imitate birds. Thus there are various ways of calling the same birds. The "ge-zuo-ge-gong" (*each does its own work*) can also sound like "gan-zao-fa-ke" (*begin work while it is early*). But in the silk producing areas in Jiangsu and Zhejiang Provinces, it turned to be "shi-shi-kan-de-hao" (*good guards for the silkworm*) because, in the local term, the silkworm is called shi-shi, and the bird becomes the guardian of the silkworm. There are certainly different versions, but I unfortunately have not directly heard them.

The garden snake is a type of small green snake in the mountains. It is not poisonous, and is common in Jiangsu and Zhejiang areas. However, my hometown may also have this kind of snake. We just never pay attention to it. This is a very popular fairy tale in my hometown, but it is not known whether it originated in our Taiping County, Anhui Province, since there are similar tales in other areas. I am not sure whether the snake tale that you talked about is similar to this one.

When I listened to my ailing mother telling this tale with a weak and gentle tone, in the lamplight shadow next to the window, I suddenly felt I returned to my childhood, full of indescribable feelings of endearing and mystery. The beauty of the tale is a different question, but the pleasure of listening to her telling is the feeling I have not had in the past decade or more, because these tales can bring in my previous pinkish twilight dreams!

Xue Lin

Letter from the editor to the contributor:

Dear Xue Lin;

The Garden Snake tale is the same as the Snake Man tale that I know of. The garden snake is also extant in Shaoxing, Zhejiang Province, and is called *caihua* snake, which sounds like *Tseeh-uoazoa*. In the fairy tale, however, it is "personified" as a young man, without any reptile trace, except that it wants to eat up the human. This change is the same as in the tale of Cinderella (*huiguniang*) in which the mother changed, due to different cultural backgrounds, from a cow to a fairy. The transformation in the later part of the tale is very similar to the oldest fairy tale in the world—the Egyptian "Tale of Two Brothers." In this tale, there is marriage between the human and the beast, transformation, and victory of the third daughter. They are important elements to form legends and myths, and all of these aspects can be compared to the primitive culture. It is one of the tales with greatest academic value. If we can collect this type of tales from different places, and get a hundred or so variants, we can do comparative studies. Those variants will not only be valuable materials in cultural history, but also make the studies interesting. We are not that ambitious to become academicians (and there is no sign of having such learning in China now), but simply for the sake of having fun it is worthwhile to do this kind of half-game work.

Some details in the Snake Man tale are different from the Garden Snake tale. When the old man went to cut wood in the mountains, he asked his daughters what they would like to have. The eldest wanted a gold flower, and the second wanted a silver flower, but the third said, "Gold flower and silver flower are not sufficient; fresh flower is what I want to wear" (*cinghoua ninghuaoa veh nengkeu; shorhuoa nurtoo noon taila*). The last two words now are pronounced with different tones.

Also, the third sister enjoyed a luxury life after she married the Snake. The eldest sister visited her and saw the magnificent house that she had never seen before, and asked why there were noises in the kitchen.

"Golden buckets and plates, silver buckets and plates, they make ding-dong sounds" (*oingdorngloen, ningdorigboren, Baang Lorng Tingtoany Shaing*).

"What is the sound from the bedroom?"

"Golden tent hooks, silver tent hooks, they make ding-dong sounds."

There are still more, but I forgot most of it. I should ask Mr. Kawashima to write out the complete tale. He may still remember it all.

The most important thing in recording these tales is to be loyal. In the regions where the standard speech is used, it is better to record word by word. For the tales from other places, they can be recorded in standard Chinese, but we should pay greatest attention to the original versions. All those tonal changes should be written down as they are, with *pinyin* to note the sound. In terms of polishing or editing, it is the worst taboo. The way that the Garden Snake is recorded is quite good, and it can be an example, because the literary value is in the original version itself. The duty of the recorder is to try to keep the original taste, nothing else. If those literary people try to use these materials to compose poems or proses, they are certainly free to do so. But that is totally a different issue, not the question for us as collectors.

Zhou Zuoren
August 20, [1929]

2. At the end of the tale "The Ghost Brother," the contributor, Sun Jiaxun, wrote this postscript:

Mr Zhao Jingshen wrote in his article, "Chinese Fairy Tales from Bai Lang" (*Wenzhou* 8 (7)), that "The five pieces selected by Bai Lang from the *Liao Zhai* . . . in my opinion, only the piece named Wang Liu Lang could be seen as a fairy tale. I have discussed with Mr Zhou Zuoren about fairy tales, and once said, 'Wang Liu Lang in *Liao Zhai* seems to be a fascinating fairy tale' (*Tonghua Lunji*, p. 68). According to *Liao Zhai*, this tale was common in Zhaoyuan, Zhangqiu and Shikengzhuan regions, but 'hard to know which version is the original one.' It seems quite fit to be a variant of the fairy tale." After I read this passage, I found and read the Wang Liu Lang tale in the *Liao Zhai*. I suddenly remembered the Ghost Brother tale that I heard in Yuntai when I was young. It was very similar to this one. But I could not recall how it was told. That afternoon, I went to ask Bald Fourth Grandpa in the mill whether he knew the Ghost Brother tale. He said yes. So, this recording is based on his telling. Hearing his telling, I recalled most of the Ghost Brother tale that Yuntai people told. Here is the outline:

There was a fisherman who built a hut along the river, living in it with his wife. Somehow, they met with a water ghost, and got along well. Thus, they became brothers, and the water ghost was the elder brother. The water ghost was in the water all the time, driving fish to the net so that the fisherman greatly benefited from this. About three years later, the water ghost said, "There will be a man crossing the river tomorrow. I need to use his body to come to a new human life." The next day, indeed, a man came over. He wanted to walk across the river. The fisherman pulled him out of the water, and said, "There is ghost in the water!" Then he told the man to cross the river from a bridge in a certain place, and the man walked away. That evening, the water ghost got on the riverbank, and said, "Younger Brother, you indeed hurt me!" Another three years later, the water ghost told the fisherman, "I will take a woman's body to come to a new life." The next day, indeed, there were two sisters-in-law who came to fetch water from the river. Because the daughter-in-law suffered from her mother-in-law, she wanted to throw herself into the river. The fisherman rushed over and held her, and asked the younger girl to persuade her sister-in-law to go back home. That evening, the water ghost rolled up the riverbank, and said, "Younger Brother, you indeed hurt me!" Another three years passed by. The water ghost passed the due time to transform to a new life. The King of Hell showed sympathy to him, and thus sent him to become a city god in a certain place. When the water ghost was to depart, he told the fisherman, "When you are in big trouble, you can look for me." Afterward, the fisherman caught less and less fish. He then went to look for his elder brother, who then told him that his wife was dying, and the only way to save her was to ask her to make pancakes for three days and three nights. This part was very much the same as the tale told by Bald Fourth Grandpa, so I will not repeat. After the fisherman's wife died, he missed her so much that he went to look for his water ghost brother for help so that he could see his wife. The ghost brother told him that his wife was now married to the butcher in hell, living in a certain place. The fisherman wanted to go to look, but the ghost brother did not agree. The fisherman insisted, then the ghost brother finally let him go to look at his wife. The fisherman arrived at the butcher's house, and saw his wife. He called her, but she did not reply. He did not want to leave. The butcher suddenly entered the house with a sharp knife in his hand. The fisherman then ran away when the butcher was chasing after him waving the knife.

There is also a tale "Little Boy as the Earth God" in the Donghai region, and it goes like this:

A boy from a rich family drowned to death in a pond. Three years later, he sent a dream to his father, and said, "There will be a person taking a bath in the pond. I will take his body to come to a new life." The next day, his father indeed saw a man walking to the pond to take a bath. His father hurried to stop the man and told him there was a ghost in the water. Three years later, the boy again sent a dream to his father, and said, "There will be a woman riding a donkey passing by the pond tomorrow. I will take her body to come to a new life." The next day, his father indeed saw a woman riding a donkey passing by the pond. Again, he stopped her and told her to take a different path. That night, the boy sent a dream to his father and said, "The King of Hell saw that you are a kind-hearted person. So he asked me to be the Earth God in this area." The next day, his father donated money to build a small temple in front of the village, and put the boy's statue in it. It is said that the Earth God was young in age, but was very effective. (This tale is provided to me by my friend Wu Luxing.)

Now that we have collected these materials, we can, on the one hand, prove Mr Zhao Jingshen's hypothesis; on the other hand, find the variants of the tale Wang Liu Lang. It is a common superstition that the drowned ghost wanted to look for a human body to transform. Maybe this superstition is the original form of the kind of tales about "looking for a human body." Later, the tale changed, either owing to the fact of his failure in finding a human body, or being kind to others (just like Wang Liu Lang), or his family members being kind to others (like this Little Boy as the Earth God), or passing the due time and being shown sympathy by the King of Hell (like the Ghost Brother), and thus became the Earth God or City God. In the tale of Wang Liu Lang, there are only two details in the plot (catching more fish and showing effectiveness) more than that of the Little Boy as the Earth God. It is obvious that the former was built upon the latter. The Ghost Brother tale told by the people in Yuntai has another two more details than Wang Liu Lang, namely, asking the woman to make pancakes and being chased by the butcher in hell. The center of the tale moved from the ghosts or gods to the human. In my opinion, among these variants, this tale is the best in terms of structural delicacy and balance of the plot. As far as the version of the Ghost Brother told by Bald Fourth Grandpa, there are three more details than the version told by the people in Yuntai: the chefs and servant transforming into immortals after eating the fish, the fisherman breaking the drum, and the fisherman killing the hairy people. Bald Fourth Grandpa said that the tale did not end at where he told, that is, the fisherman did a lot of bad things wearing the cap and red shirt from the hairy man. I think those bad things must be similar to the tale "Strange Turnip," in which Wang Bang wore the dog-fir vest to climb up to a girl's room. It would be too tedious if the tale continues like this. That the chefs and servant became immortals after eating fish is very similar to the detail in the tale "Grandpa Buddha" (see my description in *Baby Stone*), in which Zhang Guolao stole the ginseng. Putting this detail into the tale of Ghost Brother is a minutiae, and it does not fit in.

3. At the end of the tale "The Fairy Cave," the contributor, Sun Jiaxun, wrote this postscript:

> According to the *Records of the Gods and Immortals* (*Shen Xian Ji*), Liu Chen and Ruan Zhao entered the Tian Tai Mountain on the same day. They lost their way as they gathered medical herbs. They met two ladies who welcomed them to their home. The two men ate some sesame food, and then begged to go home. When they got home, they saw their

seventh-generation descendants. The current tale is a variant of the record in *Shen Xian Ji*. The story of encountering fairy ladies while fetching water is similar to the tale of Lu Lin Xiao (see the tale in my book *Baby Stone*). The fairy women gave Liu Chen and Ruan Zhao sticks for opening the cave door. This detail is similar to the tale of "Shihua County" in which Ge San got a stick to open the city gate of the Shihua County. All the plots fall in the discussion in the Chapter of "The Supernatural Lapse of Time in Fairyland" in *The Science of Fairy Tales* by Edwin Hartland. Mr Zhao Jingshen wrote in his book *Chinese Fairy Tales*, "American writer Washington Irving's *Rip Van Winkle* belongs to this type (The Supernatural Lapse of Time in Fairyland). The Grimms' The Little Shepherd Boy also belongs to this type."

Ai Bo Hua (艾伯华). 1999. 《中国民间故事类型》. 王燕生、周祖生译, 北京: 商务印书馆. [Chinese translation of Eberhard (1937b).]

Cai Shuliu (蔡漱六). 1985. 关于林兰 [About Lin Lan]. *Lu Xu Studies Monthly* (鲁迅研究月刊) 5: 45.

Che Xilun (车锡伦). 2002. 林兰"与赵景深 [Lin Lan and Zhao Jingshen]. *New Literature History* (新文学史料) 1: 36–37.

Chen Lina (陳麗娜). 2010. 中國民間故事類型研究 [The Research of Chinese Folk-Tale Types]. PhD dissertation, National East China University.

Chen Shuping (陈树萍). 2006. 北新书局：新文化运动的推动者 [North New Books: Promoter of the New Culture Movement]. *New Literature History* (新文学史料) 1: 164–170.

Ding Nai Tong (丁乃通). 1983. 《中国民间故事类型索引》. 孟慧英、董晓萍、李扬译，沈阳: 春风文艺出版社. [Chinese translation of Ting (1978).]

———. 2008. 《中国民间故事类型索引》. 郑建威等译，武汉: 华中师范大学出版社. [Revised edition, Chinese translation of Ting (1978).]

Eberhard, Wolfram. 1937a. *Chinese Fairy Tales and Folk Tales*. Trans. Desmond Parsons. London: K. Paul, Trench, Trubner.

———. 1937b. *Typen chinesischer Volksmärchen*. FF Communications no. 120. Helsinki: Suomalainen Tiedeakatemia, Academia Scientiarum Fennica.

Gao Youpeng (高有鹏). 2013. 中国现代民间文学史上的"林兰女士"与《民间故事》 ["Lady Lin Lan" and "Folk Tale" in Modern Folk

Literature History in China]. *Cultural Heritage* (文化遗产) 3: 79–87.

Hartland, Edwin. 1891. *Science of Fairy Tales: An Inquiry into Fairy Mythology*. London: W. Scoot.

Jameson, R. D. 1932. *Three Lectures on Chinese Folklore*. Peking: North China Union Language School.

Jin Ronghua (Yung-Hua King, 金榮華). 2000–2002. 中國民間故事集成類型索引(一), (二) [*An Index of Collections of Chinese Folktales (I, II)*]. 台北: 中國口傳文學學會.

———. 2003. 中國民間故事與故事分類 [*A Classification of Chinese Folktales and Tale Types*]. 台北: 中國口傳文學學會.

———. 2007. 民間故事類型索引 [*An Index of Folk Tale Types*]. Vols. 1–3. 台北: 中國口傳文學學會.

Li Liang (黎亮). 2018. 中国人的幻想与心灵：林兰童话的结构与意义 [*The Chinese Fantasy and Heart-Mind: The Structure and Meaning of Lin Lan Fairy Tales*]. Beijing: Shangwu yinshuguan.

Liu Shouhua (刘守华). 2017. 中国民间故事史 [*A History of Chinese Folktales*]. Beijing: Shangwu yinshuguan.

Qi Lianxiu (祁连休). 2007. 中国古代民间故事类型研究 [*The Study of Ancient Chinese Folk Tale Types*]. Shijiazhuang: Hebei Jiaoyu Chubanshe.

Ranke, Kurt. 1966. *Folktales of Germany*. Trans. Lotte Baumann, foreword by Richard Dorson. Chicago: University of Chicago Press.

Ting, Nai-tung. 1974. *The Cinderella Cycle in China and Indo-China*. Helsinki: Suomalainen Tiedeakatemia.

———. 1978. *A Type Index of Chinese Folktales*. FF Communications no. 223. Helsinki: Suomalainen Tiedeakatemia Academia Scientiarum Fennica.

Uther, Hans-Jörg. 2004. *The Types of International Folktales: A Classification and Bibliography Based on the System of Antti Aarne and Stith Thompson*. Vols. 1–3. FF Communications nos. 284–286. Helsinki: Suomalainen Tiedeakatemia Academia Scientiarum Fennica.

Wang Wenbao (王文宝). 2003. 中国民俗研究史 [*A History of Chinese Folklore Studies*]. Harbin: Heilongjiang Chubanshe.

Zhang, Juwen. 2018. "Folklore in China: Past, Present, and Challenges." *Humanities* 7 (35): 1–20.

———. 2019. "Fairy Tales in China: An Ongoing Evolution." In *The Fairy Tale World*, ed. Andrew Teverson. London: Routledge. Pp. 335–346.

———. 2020. "Rediscovering the Brothers Grimm of China: Lin Lan." *Journal of American Folklore* 133 (529): 285–306.

Zipes, Jack. 1987. *The Complete Fairy Tales of the Brothers Grimm*. New York: Bantam Books.

———. 2012. *The Irresistible Fairy Tale: The Cultural and Social Evolution of a Genre*. Princeton, NJ: Princeton University Press.

———. 2013. *Golden Age of Folk and Fairy Tales*. Indianapolis: Hackett.

■ Biographical Notes on Important
  Writers and Contributors

Please note that names are given here in Chinese format, with family name first.

Li Xiaofeng (李晓峰, 1897–1971): As the founder of the North New Books publishing house, which exerted tremendous influence on the social and cultural changes in the late 1920s and early 1930s, Li Xiaofeng was a representative of the progressive youth during the New Culture Movement in the early twentieth century in China. Li was a pioneer in introducing Western theories of folk literature, collecting and publishing Chinese folk literature. Through North New Books, many significant writers at that time (for example, Lu Xun, 1881–1936) published their important works. Lu Xun is known as the greatest writer of the twentieth century in China. Li Xiaofeng was a student of Lu Xun's in Peking University in the early 1920s, and later they became close friends. After the 1940s until his death, Li Xiaofeng seemed to have retreated from social and public activities, with no more records of publications.

Lin Lan (林兰): As discussed in the introduction, Lin Lan was first used as a pen name by Li Xiaofeng, and later became a collective name used by a small group of editors at North New Books, Shanghai. The small group included Li Xiaofeng and his wife, Cai Shuliu (1900–?), Zhao Jingshen, and possibly a few more people. As shown in the letter from the editor to the Xue Lin (see note 1 in the section "Bibliographic Sources and Tale Types"), it was clear that Zhou Zuoren was also one of the editors of the Lin Lan Series who might have used the name Lin Lan. For more detailed discussion, see also Zhang (2020).

Sun Jiaxun (孙佳讯, 1908–1990): Sun Jiaxun was not only an important contributor to the Lin Lan Series but also a writer, poet, and editor who separately published several volumes on folk and fairy tales. He was from Guanyun County, Jiangsu Province, where many of his tales were collected. Among a number of tales that he contributed to the Lin Lan Series, four tales (11, 39, 40, 41) are selected in this translated collection. He was regarded as an accomplished literary scholar in his hometown. In 1945 and 1948–1950, he became the principal of the Middle School of Guanyun County. In his late years, he concentrated on the investigation of the authorship of the famous literature piece *Jing Hua Yuan* (*Mirror Flower Fortune*) and provided the most convincing evidence, while there is no record of his other publications (for example, on folk and fairy tales) after the 1950s until his death in Nanjing.

In the notes to the tales "The Ghost Brother" and "The Fairy Cave" (see notes 2 and 3 in the section "Bibliographic Sources and Tale Types"), Sun provided not only some contextual information about collecting and telling those tales, but also some theoretical studies regarding the intertextuality of those tales in relation to other versions and earlier literary records. As a young man in his twenties, Sun's notes indicated that he had had sufficient education and knowledge of folk- and fairy-tale studies in the 1920s, especially his mention of the work *Science of Fairy Tales* published in 1891 by Edwin Hartland. This can also be understood as an indication of the overall situation of interests and studies of folk and fairy tales in China in the early twentieth century.

Zhao Jingshen (赵景深, 1902–1984): Zhao Jingshen is still known as one of the most important scholars of fairy-tale studies in China, with his pioneering works in translating Western fairy tales and studying Chinese fairy tales laying the foundation for the study of fairy tales in China. He is also known as a historian, educator, drama scholar, and writer. Since the 1930s, he had taught at Fudan University until his retirement. Zhao Jingshen was essential to the establishment of North New Books, and held the position of editor-in-chief of the publishing house. Many of his studies published from the 1920s to the 1980s still play an important role in such fields as folk drama, folk literature, literature history, and, particularly, fairy-tale studies. In his late years, he was elected president of the China Association of Ancient Drama Studies and honorary president of the Chinese Institute of Folk Literature, founded in 1984.

Zhou Zuoren (周作人, 1885–1967): Zhou Zuoren is perhaps the most important figure in introducing "fairy-tale studies" to China, and in promoting children's literature and women's education in China at the beginning of the twentieth century. He is known as a writer, literary critic, poet, translator, and thinker, as well as a founder of Chinese folklore studies. It may be previously unknown that Zhou Zuoren used his pen name, Qiming (启明), in replying to a contributor (see note 1 in the section "Bibliographic Sources and Tale Types," related to the tale "The Garden Snake"). This also proves that he was one of those who used the name Lin Lan as the editor of the series, showing that he was an active member of the movement of collecting and publishing folklore as an approach to promoting children's and public education in China as a key to social change in the early twentieth century.

As seen in note 1 to the tale "The Garden Snake," it was very likely that Zhou Zuoren wrote the letter with his pen name, Qiming. In the last paragraph of the letter, Zhou Zuoren mentioned that "The most important thing in recording these tales is to be loyal . . . polishing or editing [tales], it is the worst taboo. . . . The duty of the recorder is to try to keep the original taste, nothing else. If those literary people try to use these materials to compose poems or proses, they are certainly free to do so. But that is totally a different issue, not the question for us as collectors." This is a clear indication that Zhou Zuoren knew well the theoretical discussions about folklore collection in the West, including studies of folk and fairy tales like those collected by the Brothers Grimm. Indeed, twenty years earlier, Zhou Zuoren was the first person in China who introduced the concepts like "fairy tale" (*tonghua*) and "folklore" (*minsu*) to China by borrowing the Japanese characters.